BENT OATH

BENT OATH

BY

RUSSELL BESSETTE

ISBN: 9781661332631 (paperback)

To Missy because of her love, care and loyalty everything is possible.

Prologue

As Malcolm Reinhardt parked his F-Type Jaguar next to his wife's silver Mercedes, he crunched two breath mints to mask the three bourbons he'd drunk at the club. Scooping the pile of legal papers off the passenger seat, he girded himself for her ambush. Despite his eloquence in the courtroom, he quivered under her questioning. Since today was her biweekly chemotherapy for ovarian cancer, her attack tonight would be venomous.

Her first question usually began, "How's your slut tonight? Or should I say, your paralegal whore?"

The grilling always ended with a truckload of guilt; as she reminded him, he had taken an oath in sickness and in health.

However, if she, at any time, described his paralegal as a thin blonde without crow's feet, sagging breasts, and a nine-inch belly scar, then her assault was nuclear.

Gingerly opening the house door, he was smacked not by her roar but by a wave of natural gas. Choked by the pungent air, he screeched, "Jane!" But it sounded more like a whimper.

Turning to face the open garage door, a mere seventeen feet away, he sought a gulp of fresh night air. But instead of air, more gas drilled his lungs.

Propping the main door open with his pile of papers, he strode for the patio doors on the other side of the kitchen. Halfway to his goal, a flashing red light from the double oven caught his eye. As he lunged for a control knob, he stumbled over her twisted body. Dropping to a knee, he yanked her shoulder, which flipped her over like a log. The dim oven light lit her open eyes, which matched her gaping mouth. As undigested corn chips and sour whiskey crept up his throat, he swallowed them again, which amplified his thirst for air.

As he gripped the counter to stand, the room swayed from left to right. Hoping that light might clear his head, he flipped the wall switch. But like a bad bulb, the light only flickered and then unleashed a crackling sound. He rushed for the patio doors, and the sound followed him. When the sound became a flash of blue light, it launched him off the floor. As his face shattered the glass, his skin bubbled like plastic wrap in a broiling oven. Before his neighbors heard the blast, his eardrums burst, and his mind went black as the night.

Chapter 1

At Monroe General Hospital, the emergency department was quiet, until the Crips and Nomads decided to teach each other respect. Their fight mobilized trauma surgeon Dr. Susan Whitney into action. Her patient, a seventeen-year-old white male, sustained a razor blade gash, which ran from his left eye to his chin. Although the wound was scalpel clean, it missed both the facial artery and a branch of his facial nerve.

That good fortune kept him in the emergency area and avoided the need for general anesthesia. But for everyone else, it spelled trouble as the muscular boy thrashed, squirmed, and tugged at the handcuffs locking him to the treatment table. His unfettered mouth screamed; his words echoed down the corridor: "I'll kill those bastards!"

After numbing the wound with the maximum dose of Xylocaine, she irrigated his laceration with hydrogen peroxide and sterile saline. Employing a suturing technique, which would eliminate the need for a return visit, she deftly drew the wound edges together with a single long suture beneath the skin that would dissolve in two weeks.

As she taped a gauze dressing onto his face, the two cops leaning against the wall, each with folded arms sculpted by daily weight lifting, moved to either side of the table. Each cop clutched one of the kid's arms and twisted it behind his back. The would-be fugitive, intent on revenge, struggled to lift himself off the bed. As one officer wrapped his free arm around the boy's neck, the taller one, with two chevrons on his short-sleeved shirt, said, "Easy, big guy, you're coming with us."

In the boy's quest for revenge, he kicked the Mayo stand, which catapulted scissors, scalpels, and forceps into the air. Clattering to the tile floor, they bounced and hit a nurse, who scurried from the room, wiping blood off her pant leg. Both officers tightened their grip and locked the boy's arms behind his back. Yanking his arms upward as if to flip him upside down, they hauled him down the corridor, his feet dragging on the floor like flukes on a claw anchor.

As Susan removed her gloves and surgical mask, she shook her head and wondered about the boy's plight, as well as her own predicament. Normally, she would have been upstairs as the lead trauma surgeon attending to the two other warriors. One gang member had a gunshot wound that had ruptured his spleen, while the other had a knife wound that had punctured his lung and torn his liver.

But since her license was still probationary, her medical practice was restricted to minor procedures in the emergency department under the watchful eyes of her court-appointed mentor. The edict from the New York State Education Department was clear: "Before we consider reinstating your license, you must complete an alcohol rehab program followed by one year of supervised medical practice."

Her solitude broke when a nurse burst into the room and cried, "Dr. Whitney, major trauma coming in. Severe burns, airway obstruction, ETA five minutes."

Racing to the central nursing station, she stood alongside the radio operator collecting vitals from the ambulance. As the male nurse with a ponytail leaned in closer to the radio, scribbling notes, she asked, "What are the vitals?"

Pointing with his pen, he said, "BP sixty over forty, heart rate one sixty-one, deep facial lacerations with embedded glass. Estimate body burns at 40 percent. Can't be more accurate; clothes are stuck to the skin."

Leaning over the nurse's shoulder, she stared at the chart as if something was missing. Then she asked, "What happened?"

"House explosion. Burns would have been worse, but the rain—"

Suddenly, she grabbed the clipboard, causing the nurse to drop his pen as she shrieked, "Malcolm Reinhardt the malpractice lawyer?"

Stunned, the nurse mumbled, "Yeah. Maybe."

Glaring at the chart as if to vaporize his name, she tried to suppress the memories of Reinhardt raging in her mind. Just then, the radio squawked, "Pressure falling; he'll need blood, stat. Pulling into the ramp now."

Through the plexiglass enclosure, she stared beyond the crowded waiting room, out through the front doors, at the flashing red lights. As the ambulance jerked to a halt, raindrops slid down its smooth white sides. The driver, dressed in a khaki uniform, jumped out and dashed to open the rear door.

Seconds later, a metal stretcher dropped its wheels as three paramedics rolled a body covered in a blue blanket toward her.

The lead EMT called out, "Which room?"

The charge nurse snapped back, "Room two," as she scurried after them.

As the entire ER team clicked into their trauma response, her feet were fused to the floor. She knew the drill, but her legs were frozen. Then she heard, "Dr. Whitney—cardiac arrest."

As if the cry unsnapped her feet, she felt herself driven forward. Yet the memories of her brutal trial dragged behind her. The lawsuit seemed like yesterday. Yet it smoldered within her and foretold an eternity before it would end. Her every nightmare recalled each wrinkle, frown, and sneer on his disdainful face. They were chiseled forever.

Entering the treatment room, a team surrounded the narrow table. An intern pumped the chest while calling out a cadence count. The anesthesia resident struggled to slide a breathing tube down the patient's windpipe.

As if they thought she were the prophet Moses, the medical students parted to clear a path to the table. Sensing the group's stare, she wondered, did they see contempt, or were they merely anxious for her medical orders?

Dropping her gaze to study his face, she found nothing that matched her memories. Gone were the scowling creases and the raised eyebrow, along with the infernal snarling lip. Now they were replaced with cracked, charred skin that was clogged with soot, grass, dried blood, and shards of glass that projected like quills from a porcupine. His charred Zegna suit, black as a judge's robe, provided his only link back to the courtroom.

As a nurse sliced the victim's trousers with sharp silver scissors, he rubbed areas of unburnt skin, searching for a vein. After several futile attempts, he gazed upward and shrugged.

Susan called out to the charge nurse, "Get me a central line kit!"

Turning to face another nurse, whose designer glasses had slid halfway down her nose, she added, "Ready three amps of bicarb for rapid IV push."

Snapping on sterile gloves, she mentally reviewed the treatment for critical burn patients. These patients were special. Not only did their organ injuries require repair, but they needed hydration desperately. Water they lost to fire. Water trapped inside smoke-damaged lungs. It all needed replacement. Additionally, they needed food, over five thousand calories a day to fuel a frantic repair. If these requirements weren't met in the first eight hours, chances for survival were nil.

As the nurse dashed back into the room, she opened a towel-wrapped package. A twenty-cc syringe slid across a sterile towel, along with a four-inch needle. A med student with eyes that matched the deep blue of the towel tore a swatch of shirt that covered the patient's clavicle. He then painted the skin with Betadine and draped a paper sheet with a three-inch hole to encircle a target below the right collarbone.

Using two fingers, she probed the area beneath his clavicle, searching for a vein buried deep in his chest. From experience, she knew how important it was to enter the vein with the first needle strike. If there were time, this procedure would have been guided by ultrasound imaging. But this was an emergency. Clutching the syringe, she plunged the needle deep into her tormentor's chest. Gently vacillating the barrel left and right, she felt the needle's tip tickle the elusive subclavian vein. Hesitating for an instant, she guided the needle forward and then tugged on the plunger. As dark blood filled the syringe, she clamped the needle's hub with a hemostat and disconnected the syringe.

With the intern pumping the chest, blood spurted from the open needle in rhythm to his compressions. Seizing the thin plastic catheter, she threaded it through the needle into the right atrium of the heart. When the white marking dot reached her fingers, she stopped. Connecting the free end to an IV bag of Ringer's lactate, she turned and said, "Run wide open. Send this blood stat—CBC, electrolytes, and type-four units of unmatched blood."

Gazing at his EKG, she watched the little green dot lazily trace a straight flat line. Removing her bloody gloves, she snatched two defibrillator paddles from the nurse standing next to her. Exposing the metal underbellies of the paddles to a med student, she waited while he squeezed green conductive paste onto them. Mashing the paddles together, she smeared the paste like melted butter, then slapped the paddles to Reinhardt's chest. Gazing around the table to be certain no one touched it, she shouted, "Clear."

Depressing the paddle buttons with her thumbs, she blasted him with enough current to match his nastiest day. As the jolt shortened his muscles, his back arched off the table. Yet the little green dot on the monitor just trudged unfazed across the screen.

The intern shook his head and then pumped the chest with renewed vigor, while his partner squeezed the Ambu bag that inflated the lungs.

After seven chest compressions, she said, "Increase the joules to 350. Let's do it again." Then she shouted, "Clear."

This shock lifted him so high, one would have thought he was planning to leave. As before, he hit the table with a thud. But this time, the green dot, which had followed his rise, fluttered back to the baseline as if on a parachute. Once there, it shook itself as though awoken from a trance. Finally, it traced a heartbeat.

"Nice job, Doctor," whispered an EMT standing behind her.

A nurse who was seated on a stool and recording vitals called out, "Pressure rising, fifty over thirty; heart rate forty-two."

But Susan's success unmasked a problem. With a rising pressure, blood now gushed from his neck. Snapping on new gloves, she yelled, "Get a vascular tray, stat."

As a nurse in surgical scrubs scurried to the instrument cabinet, Susan gently touched the open neck wound. Feeling a hard, jagged nodule, she realized a shard of glass had cut the jugular vein. If left there, the glass might slip, and as a result, it might cut the carotid artery.

Grasping a set of vascular clamps, she said, "We can't wait for a cross-match. Prepare to transfuse two units O-negative blood."

Understanding the risk of using unmatched blood, she felt the danger of a ruptured artery outweighed it. Lifting the skin with forceps, she touched the glass as gently as a hummingbird would a flower. Still the wound responded by spurting dark blood. Convinced the jugular vein was severed, rather than an artery, she lifted the glass free. As if she'd unplugged a dam, blood gushed over his shoulder. Seizing a vascular clamp, she squeezed the upper half of the vein, which reduced the flow to a drip. Snatching another clamp, she pinched the lower half of the vein.

Deftly transecting fragments of tissue between them, she tied both ends with 3-0 silk suture. As she wiped the wound dry, the viciousness of the injury was now exposed. The carotid artery had a partial nick and would require surgical repair in the OR. Covering the wound with a saline dressing, she nodded to the nurse hanging fresh blood on an IV pole.

Removing her gloves, she reached down to palpate his bloated belly. As if her fingers were sonar, she scanned for signs of organ rupture. At that same moment, the team moved away from the table to expose Dr. Henry Taylor.

His very appearance set him apart from everyone else. Though he wore the same blue surgical scrubs as the others, his shirt and pants weren't baggy or wrinkled. Rather they were starched, perhaps even tailored. The diamond embedded in his thick gold ring sparkled beneath the gold Rolex on his wrist. It also predicted how near he would get to the patient. Even as an intern, she'd mentally divided anesthesiologists into two groups: those that treated and those that directed. Indeed, Taylor was a cruise ship director. Unfortunately for her, Taylor was also her court-appointed mentor.

"Dr. Whitney, I scanned this patient's chart and concluded he requires immediate surgery. I've called for Drs. Harrison and Cook."

"Thanks, Henry. I came to the same conclusion without reading his chart."

As the nurse adjusting the IV stifled a snicker, Taylor glared and snapped, "Doctor, step outside." Then, burning the smirking nurse with his stare, he said, "Dr. Harrison's resident will be here shortly. Call X-ray now for CT scans. Understood, Nurse?"

Strutting from the room, he said, "Doctor Whitney, a word, please." He stopped outside the doorway, pivoted, and scowled. "Do you know who that patient is?"

"I should, Henry. He put me here."

"And if he dies, his law firm will put you out of here. Since I'm responsible for your actions, why didn't you call me first?"

"Henry, he was in cardiac arrest. What would you have had me do?"

"Use better judgment, Doctor. Transfusing a patient with unmatched blood, tying off a vessel, not to mention treating someone you hate..."

Glancing down the hall, she saw Harrison's chief resident approaching, and from the look on his face, it was obvious he'd heard every word of Taylor's diatribe. Dropping his gaze to the floor, the resident scurried into the room.

Unfazed, Taylor continued, "I have no choice but to report your actions to the hospital's CEO. Now please excuse me. This patient requires coordinated care, not shotgun medicine."

Spinning on his heel, he strode to the elevator as she leaned against the wall for support. The interns lifted Reinhardt onto the transport cart and then glided past her for the express elevators. Staring at the bouncing green dot on the heart monitor, she thought it appeared to be waving goodbye. As the elevator doors closed, she wondered why good deeds were never remembered and bad ones never forgotten.

Chapter 2

Cindy Franklin awoke and stared at the tremor in her hands. Reaching for the half-filled glass of water on the nightstand, she knocked both the glass and her bottle of clonazepam to the carpeted floor. Rubbing her forehead as if to squeeze out the nightmare, she tried to cry. But she couldn't. Each night since the surgery, nightmares had plagued her. Rushing to the bathroom to see if it was worse, she stared into the mirror and found it was so. Damn him. Damn him to hell!

Grasping her toothbrush, she pumped out paste, of which only half stayed on the brush. Unable to fully open her mouth, she rammed the brush between her capped molars. Yet she couldn't stop staring at the gawking face. Her eyelids were stretched so tight, they turned her lower lids inside out. Her taut cheeks had wrinkle lines that all pointed back to her ears.

Lifting a handful of stringy blond hair that covered her ear, she exposed the incision line, now only three weeks old. The plastic surgeon said the incision in front of both ears was in a natural skin fold. The incision ran upward into her scalp and downward behind her ear. The butcher had promised, "No one will see it."

But she could see it. And now it resembled a snake. A red coral snake, which got redder each day. As a matter of fact, the snake's belly in front of her ear was swollen by a quarter inch. Tracing its body upward with her long purple nail, she searched for the snake's head. There it was. A hard, raised lump above her temple, covered with matted hair. Carefully, she withdrew her finger, fearing the snake might bite.

The so-called surgeon, who did not always answer her daily calls, said the lump was where he had placed a surgical drain. But the drain was gone now, and the lump was still there. The lying bastard was afraid to tell her: it was a snake. Sliding her finger behind her ear, she felt the snake's tail. Tracing its cool body, she held her finger very still. There it was. She was certain. The steady thumping. The snake was alive and growing.

Her devious surgeon argued that the scar wasn't a snake. "It's a rare face-lift complication," he said. He used a medical term to fool her, calling it a "hypertrophic scar." The liar even said, "We just need to inject the scar with cortisone after a few months of healing."

Screaming out loud, she said, "Like I'm going to let that butcher touch me again. How dumb does he think I am?"

Dropping her handful of unwashed hair, the snake vanished beneath the dark roots. And then she wondered what it ate and whether the nightmares came when it crawled inside her ear.

Still staring at the leering reflection, she watched toothpaste dribble between distorted, Botox-filled lips. As the foamy drool reached her chin, she slapped the mirror with both palms and screamed, "Damn him to hell! I was somebody once. I'm still going to sue. Even though my lawyer doesn't believe me. But I bet that slimeball is sorry now."

As she buried her hideous face in her hands, she felt tears washing down her cheeks. Why would no one listen? The snake was real. It was controlling her mind. If no one would listen and do something, she would get revenge. And the snake would tell her how to do it.

Fleeing the bathroom, she ran through the corridor and down the thickly carpeted stairs. Clutching the curved wooden banister, she headed for the front door. Carefully sliding the sheer curtain from the narrow window, she peeked onto the porch. Spying no one, she scanned the sidewalk. It was empty. She turned the dead bolt, and it clicked. Ever so cautiously, she yanked the thick wooden door ajar. Then, on her knees, peering through the slit, she scanned the porch again. Spotting no one, she opened it just wide enough to snatch the morning paper off the welcome mat.

Bolting the door, she tore apart the paper like kindling. For the past week, his story had been headline news. But today, it was half a column on page

A-eight. The police assumed that Mrs. Reinhardt, depressed with cancer, had committed suicide and triggered the massive gas explosion, which also maimed her wayward husband. The article said that police and fire inspectors were still gathering evidence.

The article went on to report Reinhardt's condition. It was critical, but he was expected to live. In sanitized language, the article suggested his burnt face was now deformed like hers. Crushing the paper between clawed hands, she screeched, "Now maybe he'll understand my condition."

Tossing the wadded paper onto the floor, she raced for the phone on the small wooden table. Punching in a number, she called Reinhardt's junior partner. Waiting for the first ring, she hoped he would understand what she meant by the word revenge.

Chapter 3

Last night, other than several patients with sprains, two with hand lacerations, and one with a fractured jaw from a barroom brawl, the surgical emergency department was quiet. Taking advantage of the quiet, Susan caught spurts of sleep in the doctors' on-call room. With an entire day off duty, she planned a morning workout at the gym, chicken salad at the deli, and some light reading at home. But once she reached her locker, the pink note taped to the gray metal door predicted a problem.

Peeling the note away, she scanned its header: From the Desk of John Friedman, CEO. The handwritten note said, "Please come to my office immediately."

After a shower in water that hadn't reached the right temperature, she brushed the wrinkles from her fresh blue blouse and tan khakis and headed for the first floor. She assumed Dr. Taylor's threats had triggered this invitation. Upon entering the administrative wing, she gazed around the circular layout of mahogany desks occupied by impeccably dressed assistants, mostly young females about her age. All of their eyes were glued to their computers as their manicured fingers glided across the keyboards. Walking to the end of the room toward the gold sign signaling the CEO's suite, she spotted his middle-aged personal assistant, who had a tinge of gray in her cropped auburn hair. With her face partially hidden behind her computer, the assistant glanced upward, and then, like a frightened deer, she leaped up and said, "Oh! Dr. Whitney, they're waiting for you."

Susan saw the conference room door was open. The knot in her throat swelled.

At the end of the polished table, which was surrounded by ten deeply padded, high-backed black leather chairs, sat CEO Friedman. Flanking his left side were Henry Taylor, who glared at her while holding a roll of papers, and Dr. Philip Harrison, chief of surgery. Across from them, seated as if marooned, was a middle-aged man wearing a black suit, blue shirt, and green tie. Although his attire was unique, it was the stack of blue-backed legal papers that drew her attention.

As Friedman gazed up, he said, "Ah...Dr. Whitney, please sit down. We've been waiting." The last statement came with a deliberate tap on his gold watch.

Expecting they wanted an apology for the time it took her to shower, she said, "I'm sorry, I was—"

Taylor, peering over his reading glasses, snapped, "Please, let's not hear another excuse. Let's move on. I have surgery in twenty minutes."

Friedman waved his arm and said, "Let me introduce Peter Regan, the hospital's attorney."

After stretching across the table to shake the lawyer's hand, she took a seat. Friedman continued, "Dr. Whitney, let's get right to the point. We're concerned about probable litigation regarding your treatment of Malcolm Reinhardt. We haven't been sued yet, but there have been inquiries."

Taylor said, "The other day in the intensive care unit, I overheard Reinhardt's sister discussing you." Curling his upper lip, he added, "And not in adoring terms."

Freidman interjected. "As you may or may not know, Mr. Reinhardt's sister is an attorney. A litigation attorney. As CEO, it's my responsibility to be concerned."

Dr. Harrison fidgeted as he leaned forward. "For Christ's sake, the patient is still in the hospital, and we're already preparing for a lawsuit? Should I stop treating him? Should I call off Dr. Cook, our plastic surgeon, to stop reconstructing his face?"

Peter Regan shook his index finger and said, "Doctors, as the hospital's attorney, I must say it's wise to be prepared." Then pointing at Susan, he added, "She's a risk, and everyone knows it."

Feeling like an object of scorn, she said, "I wish you wouldn't refer to me in the third person. I'm right here. Talk to me, not about me." Her voice rose.

"And while we're at it, let's admit you can't understand why I saved Reinhardt's life, despite hating his guts."

Dr. Harrison tried, as was his nature, to be the voice of reason. Gazing at her with blue eyes beneath stately, graying eyebrows, he said, "Sue, please don't talk like that; it's dangerous. I know—"

"Doctors, we're not here to debate her medical care," Attorney Regan said. "We're here to protect the hospital. Let's remember who lost her license and had a feud with Reinhardt."

Glaring at him, she snapped, "Look, it wasn't a feud. He represented a crooked congressman who owned a shady laboratory. I was acquitted, but his client, Congressman Rye, was censured. Furthermore, when I testified before a congressional committee investigating HMO abuses, CNN praised my actions on national news."

Regan sneered. "Correct, Doctor, you had a moment of glory. But then, after your grandiose appearance, what happened next?"

She watched Dr. Harrison's gaze drop to the table and felt as though Regan had slapped her. Friedman and Taylor smirked.

Remembering the twelve steps, she stammered, "I had a problem, but I addressed it."

Curling his lip to expose a canine, Regan said, "That's right, Doctor, and you still have a problem, don't you? You were sued after your fleeting moment of stardom. Sued by a patient who hired Malcolm Reinhardt, the very same attorney you insulted in your glamorous appearance before Congress." He shuffled his legal papers. "Doctor, what goes around comes around. Twenty-eight days in rehab doesn't change a thing."

Friedman stood and gathered his papers. "Well, gentlemen, we all have appointments." Glaring at her, he added, "Dr. Whitney, we've decided perhaps a leave of absence is in order. We won't make it official and escort you from the hospital. Unless you ignore our request. In other words, if you stay home, our decision won't make your case worse." He raised an eyebrow. "That'll give us some breathing room. Understood, Doctor?"

When everyone else stood, she felt like a broken pawn on a discarded chessboard. Leaving the room, Taylor wrapped his arm around Freidman's shoulders and asked, "See you this Saturday for golf?"

Only Dr. Harrison lingered. Clearing his throat, he said, "Sue, I'm sorry. A chief of surgery today isn't what it used to be years ago. Perhaps if…"

As his voice trailed, he adjusted his watch. "I'm sorry. I really need to go."

Staring at the polished mahogany table, she could almost see her reflection as she recalled another room like this one. That room, two years ago, was adjacent to the judge's chamber, but it served the same purpose: to isolate her while others decided her fate.

Chapter 4

Lying naked in his special hospital bed, Malcolm Reinhardt still felt on fire. The memory of that rainy night filled him with jumbled snapshots of the kitchen, the gas stove, the searing heat, and questions of who had done it. The pictures in his mind weren't right. Something was missing. But he couldn't recall what it was. Maybe if the pain would stop, he might sort it out.

It was eight days since the fire, and now his skin was a patchwork of dead black leather. The doctors called it "eschar."

Barely able to turn his head, he gazed down on his chest, which resembled a turtle shell. The cracked, corrugated skin resembled dry clay and oozed green pus from between each fissure. To prevent infection, they had taken him to surgery and cut away the burnt tissue until they reached fresh, bleeding dermal skin. Using his legs as skin farms, they harvested grafts to cover the bleeding wounds. But he needed more skin than his legs could grow.

After the surgical excision, they'd used a crane to lower him into his special bed, which the company called a Clinitron. But to him it resembled a deep bathtub, or more accurately a casket. The nurse said the bed was technically called an air-fluidized bed and that it was used to prevent friction on his sensitive skin. The bed contained nearly a ton of silicone-coated beads, each as tiny as a grain of sand. High-pressure pumps continuously blew air into the loosely packed beads. The net result was that he floated in a sea of sand-like particles with only a gossamer-thin nylon sheet keeping the beads inside the tub while allowing filtered air to wash his fragile, oozing flesh.

Despite this engineering marvel, it still was a casket that immobilized him. Unable to turn, he sank into the conforming sand between sidewalls so high even an athlete couldn't have crawled out. The tub's high gunwales permitted him to view only the ceiling. Since all doctors, nurses, and visitors were required to wear caps, masks, and gowns, everyone looked the same as they peered over the bed's edges.

The infernal air pump that kept him afloat also kept him awake. When it was added to the din of his ventilator, he needed two shots of Nembutal to sleep. Though he tried to ignore the sounds, he was powerless to control anything else.

As a matter of fact, he didn't even control his breathing. His bowels obeyed the nurse, who injected his feeding tube with a fatty liquid diet three times a day. The result was diarrhea within an hour. Altogether, along with the tube in his bladder, he controlled nothing except his perfect vision, which was now only good for staring at the ceiling.

Fortunately, the fire had spared his sight, and he thanked God for that. In college, the navy had discovered his twenty-ten eyesight. They'd hounded him to be a pilot. But his sights were set on law school, not enemy planes. And besides, everyone knew great trial lawyers didn't wear glasses. They stared directly into the jury's eyes.

Confined to his immobile shell, he had only one goal, which was to save his mind. Therefore, using his vision and love of geometry, he devised a game. Employing the respirator as a metronome, he timed how long it would take him to rearrange ceiling tile patterns into triangles, trapezoids, pentagons, hexagons, and even nonagons. Besides passing time, the game had another advantage: if the shape was complex, he grew fatigued, and merciful sleep soon followed.

But sometimes, even the game wasn't under his control, like now. As a masked nurse leaned over him, he knew what to expect. The fire had shriveled his upper lids into rolled-up shades, exposing his eyeballs like headlights. It threatened to dry out his corneas. So every few hours, a nurse lubricated them with a squirt of clear ophthalmic jelly.

Using her best baby-talk voice, the young nurse with green-as-mint eyes said, "Malcolm, how are we feeling today?"

A nod was all he could manage.

Cooing, she said, "That's OK; I know it hurts. Lie still now."

As her gloved hands swept over the gunwales, her fingers dangled like legs on an octopus, and she sang, "Time to lubricate those eyes."

As the thick jelly worm spurted from the tube, he felt it land on the center of each eye. For his bravery, she chirped, "Good boy. What a trooper."

Then, as quickly as she'd come, she vanished. Unable to blink, he felt the jelly sit like a snowdrift in western New York, waiting for spring to melt. After seventeen breaths, he felt as if he were underwater and wearing a leaky face mask. It made him recall happier times, like the scuba trips in the Cayman Islands. Through the watery haze, he imagined striped angelfish gliding between tubes of pink coral. His respirator began to mimic the sound of exhaled bubbles from his regulator. It all made him relax.

With his vision so blurry, he hardly noticed a new masked face floating above him. When a gloved hand took shape, he recognized a needle and syringe. Assuming it was time for his pain shot, he yearned for the sleep of morphine.

But the needle was terribly off course. Generally, the nurse injected him in the upper part of his leg. But this needle was swimming straight for his right eye. The closer it got, the more it resembled a silver barracuda. And like all barracudas, it stopped to hover in his watery gaze. He remembered how barracudas could do that, float stone still while flashing their crooked teeth, teeth too big for their mouths. This one was so close he couldn't see teeth. But when it bit, he felt them.

He had consoled himself that after three days in burn therapy he would never feel worse pain. But he was wrong. As daggers shot to the center of his skull, his eye socket became a cauldron of liquid fire. He opened his mouth to scream, but of course, it was useless. His air never passed his vocal cords and instead escaped through his tracheotomy tube. His silent screams now threw the respirator out of sync. That triggered a head-on collision with the machine's more powerful incoming blast. As the two air masses collided in his lungs, he convulsed with yet another new pain. With each contortion, he sank deeper into the sand until his limbs were lead.

With his good eye, he watched the barracuda wiggle free, dragging flimsy red streamers behind it. One might have thought it had stepped in bubble gum. As it swam for his left eye, it hovered and then lunged. At first, this bite was painless, almost as if the monster carried Novocain. But when the deep nerves of his skull exploded, this pain was different. He saw it. It was absolute black. Not black like inside a dark cave. It was pure, deep black. A black so dark he wondered if God was frightened when he roared, "Let there be light."

And then he understood—he was blind.

Chapter 5

When Susan left Friedman's office, she lost her former enthusiasm and just wanted to be alone. The perfect place was the doctors' meeting room at the rear of the cafeteria. Since the interns and residents were in the OR, the small windowless room was vacant. Cradling her coffee, she questioned her feelings. After all, the hospital had real concerns. Recalling her lessons from rehab at Hazelden, she was grateful for the job the hospital had given her when she was so desperate. And besides, cruel fate must have played a part by putting her and Reinhardt in the wrong place at the wrong time. Maybe a little time off was wise. Yet Peter Regan made her cringe. He was a younger, thinner, more arrogant version of Reinhardt. Taking his advice might be construed as admitting guilt. Damn the world of lawyers!

She jumped when someone tapped her shoulder. Turning, she recognized Ray Dreskin, who said, as he almost dropped his tray, "I'm sorry, Sue! Didn't mean to scare you."

Regaining his balance and composure, he asked, "Mind if I sit?"

"Go ahead. I was in a fog."

Sitting opposite her, he slid his tray of two scrambled eggs, rye toast, and coffee onto the table. "I'm surprised you're still here."

Gazing through the doorway into the empty cafeteria, she glanced at her watch. It was almost nine forty-five.

"Yeah, I must have lost track of time. Had a busy ER last night." Sipping her cold coffee, she asked, "Anyway, what brings you here?"

Dropping a fork full of egg onto a triangle of toast, he said, "Needed to see a patient and thought I'd get breakfast before going to the office."

She swirled her coffee over a few bottom grinds. "I often see your partner in the ER."

"Yeah, Tom likes trauma. Doesn't bother him staying up all night." As he blew across his cup, seeking the perfect temperature, the smell of vanilla beans was strong. Then he added with a smile, "But as for me, I enjoy sleep."

She smiled back. "That's one advantage of an all-cosmetic practice."

"Yup, that's true."

While his gaze was turned downward, she studied his chiseled face with sky-blue eyes, narrow lips, and tan skin over a sculptured nose and tiny chin cleft. Many female nurses chattered this was the main reason why a national magazine had named him one of America's top fifty cosmetic surgeons. But his jealous colleagues countered that he had bought that designation. Perhaps, she thought, it's true what they say: American women will pay anything to look as good as their plastic surgeon.

Chewing his toast, he said, "Tom told me you saved Reinhardt's life."

"I helped." Then she asked, "Did he tell you how Reinhardt is doing?"

He shook his head. "Not really, but I guess the scumbag will make it, since doctors treat lawyers better than they treat us." After a pause, he added with a tone of compulsion, "I mean, I do want him to live. Doctors do take an oath."

With a tinge of sarcasm, she said, "That's good of you."

He continued unfazed. "Look. I know the expected answer, but honestly, I hope he lives to suffer. The pain he's caused for both doctors and patients is unforgiveable. You know that better than any of us."

Not wanting to go down that path, she gulped the last swig of coffee and slid the cup across the table. "Let's hope he does well."

As if to console her, he blurted, "You're better than I am, Sue. I'm pissed because he's suing me over a crazy patient."

Pushing her chair back, she felt obliged to ask, "What happened?"

"Oh, I did a face-lift on a crazy woman, and she developed some hypertrophic scars that I can fix."

"And that's why she's suing you?"

"No. The crazy part is she thinks the scar has warped her mind. As if she has a mind." He caught his breath. "But the real insane part is that she believes the scar is a snake."

Susan's mouth fell open. "Are you putting me on?"

"No! Damn straight. When I suggested a psychiatrist, she went berserk and hired Reinhardt."

"I'm sorry, Ray. But maybe you should've involved a psychiatrist before surgery. You know most cosmetic patients are crazy."

Wiping his lips with a napkin, he answered, "Yeah, that's what all you general surgeons say until you get wrinkles."

She stood. "Well, nice chatting, Ray, but I need to get some sleep."

As she stepped out of the conference room into the cafeteria, she spotted Friedman escorting two gentlemen through the main entrance. She didn't recognize the strangers, but judging from their glares, something was wrong.

When Friedman saw her, his expression hinted at panic. Approaching her, he blurted, "I thought we told you..."

"Who's this?" the shorter gentleman asked.

"This is Dr. Susan Whitney, a staff physician who works in our emergency department."

A flash of recognition swept the taller man's face, reminding her of the stares she sometimes got from strangers who recalled her TV appearance. Extending his hand, he said, "Doctor, I'm Special Agent Jack Monihan, FBI." He wagged a thumb toward his colleague. "You might already know University FBI Task Force Officer Jeffrey Stuhl."

Shaking both their hands, she said, "No. We've never met before."

Pointing to a chair, Officer Stuhl said, "This morning, we had a problem, and we'd like some information."

She remained standing. "Maybe I've watched too much TV, but can I see your credentials?"

With a glare, Officer Stuhl unbuttoned his jacket, revealing a portly belly, and flipped open a leather wallet, which he thrust at her face. She studied the pudgy facial image beneath bold letters: University Police. Snapping the wallet back as if it were pornography, he stepped backward. His colleague, in a more gentlemanly manner, proffered his photograph, which was printed beneath the more recognizable logo of the FBI.

As Stuhl pulled out a chair, he gestured that he wanted everyone to sit. Plucking a notebook from his jacket, he clicked his pen. "Doctor, when did you get off duty?"

Adopting a posture she recalled from several cross-examinations by congressional staffers, she answered, "My usual time. Seven o'clock."

"Is it customary to hang around this long?"

Stuhl glanced at Friedman, who responded, "We had a meeting this morning."

"I see." He turned to face Freidman. "How long did that take?"

"It was over by 7:45."

Refocusing his glare back at her, he pointed to the conference room and asked, "You've been in there all this time?"

"Yes, I have. Now what's this all about?"

He ignored her question. "Please, Doctor, can anyone verify the length of time you've been here?"

Sternly she repeated, "Look, what's this all about?"

As if the encounter were staged, Ray Dreskin walked out from the conference room and said, "Excuse me, I couldn't help but overhear your conversation." He extended his hand from beneath a cardboard food tray. "I'm Dr. Raymond Dreskin. And yes, I can vouch that Dr. Whitney has been with me all morning."

Turning a page in his notebook, Stuhl said, "Could you spell your name, Doctor?"

While Stuhl scribbled a note, she studied Dreskin's poker face.

Closing his notepad, Stuhl said, "Thank you, Doctors. We may need to contact both of you again."

In a voice exposing a tinge of an Irish accent, Special Agent Monihan said, "In answer to your question, someone tried to kill Malcolm Reinhardt this morning. Given past events, Detective Stuhl has asked that the FBI investigate this matter as a hate crime. And so, Dr. Whitney, I'm certain you'll understand that we may need to speak again."

The three men stood and strode toward the door with Friedman in tow.

As Dreskin turned toward the tray conveyor belt, she grabbed his arm and said, "Why did you lie for me, Ray?"

"You've had enough trouble. I just couldn't stand to see those bastards screw you again. I don't trust Freidman. He's all company with little concern for doctors. And as for the university mall cop calling in the FBI, I say to hell with them too."

As he walked beneath the red exit sign, she wondered when her entanglement in Reinhardt's web would end. And now, just like when it had all begun, she needed his help desperately. Despite their past disagreements, Andy Falcone was still the best defense lawyer in town. Unfortunately, this time she had more baggage.

Chapter 6

With the tip of his right little finger, the only one without numbness, Malcolm touched the Xeroform dressing that plugged the hole in his throat. Four weeks since the explosion, three weeks into blindness, this morning the doctors had finally removed the tracheotomy tube so he could speak. With that milestone, he had been moved into a regular hospital bed without a noisy pump and a room without monitors covering a wall. Running his finger up and down his right cheek, he felt the wrinkled skin. He traced the large crater that was formerly his ear but then plucked his finger away for fear it might get stuck. He knew his inner ear worked because he heard doctors congratulating themselves on saving his hearing. But alas, they'd lost the outer ear. Feeling his left cheek now, he realized they should have said *ears*.

To stimulate his appetite, the doctors had added an antidepressant to his list of pain pills, antibiotics, anti-nausea meds, vitamins, and whatever else he swallowed on command. He chased away every social worker and psychologist sent to his room. Of course, he was depressed. Who wouldn't be? The life he'd known was now shattered.

To console himself, he thought of his uncle George's determination to fight pancreatic cancer. His warrior uncle had undergone surgery, a pancreatectomy, and six months of grueling chemotherapy. Yet the cancer had recurred. Malcolm recalled their conversations in hospice. His uncle had described how cancer and the certainty of death had refashioned his outlook on life. Nearing his life's end, Uncle George's sole craving was God's forgiveness. Past deeds, glories, wealth, and fame all vaporized. Instead they were replaced by feelings of compassion, forgiveness, and love for those he'd offended or family and friends he'd slighted.

But as hard as Malcolm tried, the shock of his trauma consumed him. Compassion, love, and forgiveness were converted to indifference, animus, and revenge. Touching his maimed face again, he wondered if anyone would ever speak to him without feeling revulsion. He recalled a favorite saying from a law partner: "If there's no downside to screwing you, then people will do it again and again."

Of course, civilized people would never say he looked like a monster. Even though he'd once heard a night nurse whisper that he was one. But he also knew that money bought people's allegiance. And he had wealth, plenty of it. Freshly minted cash would buy compassion, love, and forgiveness. So he vowed to only befriend sycophants.

A knock on his door broke his trance. The voice of the policeman assigned to protect him said, "Mr. Reinhardt, they've called from downstairs. Your sister will be up shortly."

His sister, Grace, had become his rock. She gave him strength, comfort, and most importantly a goal to live for. She had been at his side during his first days in the hospital. And since that day, she'd never left his side. As youngsters, they had been inseparable, but surprisingly the accident had drawn them even closer. At thirty-eight years of age, she was three years younger, yet he was still her role model. Following his graduation from Yale, she envied his acceptance to Stanford law and vowed to follow him.

Like him, she specialized in medical malpractice. And also like him, she'd placed work ahead of her marriage, which had lasted a mere two years. In similar fashion, she had no children. Their only difference was her desire to remain in California while he returned to upstate New York. A problem she pressured him to fix. She pleaded they network coast-to-coast offices under the Reinhardt name. As the years passed, she strived to preserve it. In fact, she displayed it everywhere. On his last visit to Los Angeles, he'd been greeted by a billboard five miles from LAX. Her perfect smile beneath hazel eyes was set off by her blond hair in a bouncy bob. Not only did her face brighten the ad, but it conveyed confidence to chew up doctors and spit out chunky awards. Most important to him now, she fortified his decision to seek vengeance on those who abused him.

Anxious to show off his new voice, he listened for her entrance. Before he could speak, she rushed in and said, "Malcolm, they're in panic mode. Real panic."

"What happened?"

With a pause, she gasped, "Wow, you can talk! Damn clear too." She patted his deformed hand, which was hidden beneath the sheet. "I just had a meeting with Friedman. What a jerk."

As her chair scraped across the floor, her voice grew louder. As she drew closer, he asked, "So tell me, what did he say?"

"First off, he's terrified as to what we'll do next. His inept lawyer, Peter Regan, was speechless."

Interrupting her, he said, "Never heard of him."

Then he felt a sharp pain as she plopped a weight against his hip. Hearing the zipper grind open, he recognized her leather briefcase. The one he'd given her for graduation from law school.

"These are the papers I served. We demanded all records on everyone who treated you. And by the way, both Monihan and that university cop received the same papers." She rustled more papers. "Plus I demanded to know why an alcoholic doctor had unsupervised access to you. A drunk who hates lawyers. A drunk who has past hatred for you. Who humiliated you on national news."

Facing her, he imagined she was smiling as he said, "That's good, very good. Now swear we'll make them pay."

She squeezed his hand, the one doctors said would be permanently clawed. "Don't worry. I swear they'll feel more pain than they can bear."

Turning his face toward the heat from the window, he felt splotches of sunlight on islands of normal skin. Ironically heat, despite the pain it had brought, was now becoming his friend. Rotating his head in small circles, he exposed every tiny ungrafted patch. He sighed and said, "I couldn't go to Jane's funeral. They took that away from me. They also impaired my mind."

"What do you mean?"

"Grace, there's this nagging feeling. I can't even describe it. But there's something missing from what I recall before the explosion."

"Malcolm, be patient. It'll come to you with time. You're still recovering."

He exhaled through his tightly pursed lips, and said, "I know you're right. But it worries me." Then after a pause, he added, "Just promise me again. It's payback time."

As she squeezed his hand tighter, it felt like the scars in his gnarled fingers cracked. "I swear we'll get them. As for Jane's funeral, I arranged everything. It was a small, beautiful service." After a pause and a swallow that he could hear, she added, "Like you, I'm concerned about how she died. The official report states suicide. The explosion was from gas released from a deliberately cut pipe to the ovens. According to the fire marshal, a spark was the ignition. Where it came from, no one is sure."

"It doesn't make sense, Grace. She was fighting ovarian cancer, and it seemed like she was beating it. Something just isn't right, I know it. We may need to engage one of our private detectives. I don't trust the local cops."

Never had he felt such rage, but then he recalled the words of his law school professor: "Never let emotions cloud your case."

As he turned his face away from the sun, he felt a shiver scurry down his spine. Fearing it foretold defeat, he couldn't control his desire to cry. But the doctors had warned him that was impossible. The battery acid had burned everything, including the tear glands and ducts. Releasing his hand from her grasp, he dragged his good fingertip up to the side of his nose and discovered dryness, which proved they were right. There were no tears. Yet how could that be? He was crying as hard as he could.

Chapter 7

An hour had passed, and Cindy began to fidget in the hard wooden chair. He was late, which she knew was deliberate. Rubbing her hands to control the tiny tremor, she tugged the black scarf covering her head and stretched it over her cheeks. Peeking at the gentleman reading a sports magazine in the opposite corner, she lifted the scarf to cover her lips. He mustn't see her face.

When the door to the inner office opened, a portly woman in her late forties, dressed in a beige business suit, said, "OK, Cindy, Mr. Peller will see you now. But he wants you to know that you don't have an appointment, and he only can spare a moment." To assuage the man in the corner, the assistant raised her voice and said, "But you told us it was an emergency, so we squeezed you in."

Following the assistant down the corridor, which was lined with framed newspaper articles for substantial legal awards, Cindy wondered, Where is my swift justice? She suffered while the guilty man was free. Yet their TV commercials bellowed, "Injured? Need a lawyer? Get justice with Reinhardt, Peller, and White."

Her justice was now past due. Four weeks ago, he had said, "I promise we'll help you, Cindy." However, his words were hollow. Licking the metallic taste off her teeth, she vowed to give him one more chance. She just hoped he didn't fail.

As the assistant pointed to Peller's office, she snapped, "Take a seat. Mr. Peller will see you shortly."

Plopping into the soft leather chair, she wondered, Where's the coffee? Was she getting the bum's rush? Her case would bring in millions. Money they'd enjoy while she would agonize. Whatever the outcome, her life was ruined, and they couldn't even give her a cup of coffee.

When Peller entered the room, he was carrying an armful of folders. Depositing them on the desk, he said, "Cindy, I didn't expect you back so soon. There's nothing new with your case." Taking the chair behind his desk, he tapped the pile. "Your records were destroyed in the fire at Mr. Reinhardt's home. I needed to get copies. That takes time. You need to be patient."

"That's easy for you to say, Mike. Do you bear my agony?"

"Cindy, please understand we're doing the best we can. My partner nearly died. Our entire office is in disarray. We implore your patience."

"Time is something we don't have, Michael. Your delay lets that butcher Dreskin deform other innocent women. Why don't you schedule that EBT thing? That would help."

Rubbing his forehead with a fist, he said, "You're rushing things. We don't even know if we're going to trial. An examination before trial is premature. And as I've told you, a jury may not see your face the same way you do."

Standing up, she began to pace from side to side in the narrow room, wondering what he didn't see. Then she said, "I don't have time for this. Can't you serve him with any court papers?" Halting her pacing, she faced him and lifted her scarf so he could see the snake. Which she hoped was also angry. Taking two steps forward, the snake a mere foot away from his face, she said, "Are you or are you not going to help me?"

As he jumped up and placed his hands on his narrow waist, he glared back. "Cindy, there's very little we can do right now. Furthermore, I must tell you that Dr. Dreskin's lawyer called. He reports someone is making harassing calls to the doctor's home. They suspect you. If this continues, they threaten a police report."

Her scarf nearly slipped off her face as she screeched, "I didn't call. He's calling me. Every day. He says things like, 'How do you feel, bitch? How's the snake, you whore?'" Stepping back, she pulled the scarf tightly across her face. "Maybe I called once. But it was to tell him to stop." Turning her head away, she added, "Anyway, at least his number is listed, unlike yours, Mike."

"Cindy, the doctor claims his caller ID confirms you called him."

Pacing around her chair in a circle, she pulled the scarf over her eyes, and then, staring through its silky pores at his gauzy, lying face, she said, "You don't believe me, do you?"

Walking to the door, he leaned against the frame. "Cindy, you need to leave. You have an appointment with me in four weeks. We should have more information by then." He stepped outside the doorway and called to his assistant. "Joyce, can you bring in my next appointment?"

Turning back, he shook his head. "Please be patient, Cindy. You'll be fine. And please, as we discussed, follow up with your family doctor. It's not normal to feel so uptight."

Stiffening her back, she strode past him and spat, "Sure, just what I need—another doctor, another butcher. They all stick together. They all say, 'Your face is healing fine, Cindy. You look great, Cindy.' Yeah, fine for them, not me."

When Cindy entered the waiting room, the secretary turned her head away and swiftly ushered in the waiting gentleman, who walked with a limp. As they both trudged down the corridor, she heard the assistant say, "Please, Mr. Frei, can I get you coffee or perhaps tea? Or would you like a soft drink? We're so sorry for the delay."

Watching them troop into Peller's office, she thought, They aren't sorry. They only want billable hours. Fees they earn from the pain of others. Then she stopped. The waiting room was empty, and the computer on the secretary's desk displayed a telephone contact list. Approaching the desk, she leaned back and peered down the hallway. She saw the assistant dash from Peller's office into what she assumed was the snack room. Glancing again at the monitor, then the mouse, she dove for the seat behind the keyboard. A flick of the mouse positioned the cursor on the Ps. One more click and a nudge of the scroll bar exposed "Peller, Michael J." Her double click brought up his personal information. And there it was: a hacker's dream.

Staring at the monitor, she mused how nice it must be to have a secretary book your flights, buy gifts for a new client referral, or make sure you never forgot a birthday or anniversary. Someone to polish the image of a caring lawyer. Lifting a pencil off the immaculate desk, she copied the sixteen digits of his Visa card, along with its code and expiration date, onto a yellow sticky note. Then she jotted his address and telephone number, the one with the notation "unlisted." She ripped off the sheet and closed the pop-up window. Streaking through the exit door, she wrapped the scarf across her face and whispered aloud, "You'll be hearing from me, Mike. Sooner than you think."

Chapter 8

Seated next to Andy outside the conference room for the hospital board of directors, Susan felt a shadowy sense of doom begin to take shape. If he weren't there, panic surely would follow. Diverting her attention, she gazed at the eight-foot-tall Howard Miller grandfather clock, then studied the walls covered with oil paintings of past chairmen of the board. She wondered when, if ever, a woman's portrait would appear.

Last week's certified letter threatened her career path. Beneath carefully chosen words, the letter carried a subliminal message that hinted the hospital and university might fire her. Of course, it didn't say that outright. Instead it declared that the hospital's credential committee wanted to clarify issues about her probationary license.

Desperate for help, she had called the only lawyer she knew: Andy Falcone, whose number was still listed under her favorites. Recalling how she'd kicked him out of her life upon entering alcohol rehab at Hazelden, she wasn't sure he would answer. But he did and, as expected, without a tone of reprisal. Hearing her concerns, he suggested an office meeting. Their first meeting was short. But two days later, they met again. Familiar with the facts, he counseled her on their gravity. Since she had been questioned by the FBI, he feared possible criminal charges. Despite their past romantic relationship, he had never discussed his work. Thankfully, she'd learned that Andy was a federal criminal defense lawyer. That led him to say now, "I really don't think you should attend this meeting. Let me go instead."

"No," she insisted. "It sends a message: I did something wrong. Which I didn't."

"Sue, it's not a question of right or wrong. These people are not your friends. If the agenda is to build a criminal charge, then loss of hospital privileges or your license is nothing compared to a criminal indictment."

With an imploring gaze, she said, "Let's compromise. Let's both go. I'll make them see the truth. And if I can't, you can take over."

Shaking his head, he answered, "All right. But choose your words carefully. The fewer the better, especially if the meeting is recorded or if a federal officer is present. Best you defer to me."

As she focused on the calming rhythm of the clock's pendulum, she noted the time. They were twenty minutes early for a nine o'clock meeting. While Andy rustled through papers within his open briefcase, she wondered if her pride had brought them here. Could things have been different? Her path to destruction and then sobriety had been rocky. But before it began, she'd sought professional help. However, no psychiatrist took her seriously. Most of them, like many doctors, didn't consider a Manhattan or two after work a problem. Everyone needed to relax. But all too soon, she'd needed more than a little to relax. Her internist believed that alcoholics were people who couldn't hold down a job. She had a job. Therefore, he said, her situation only required willpower. He advised her, "Buck up. Just stop after two drinks."

She tried that advice, but it didn't work, except for one six-day period. Soon, she needed a morning nip. Just one shot to settle her nerves. Not every morning, and never before surgery. Just on days when she needed to sit through a boring university conference. It wasn't a big deal. A drink kept her sharp. She had control.

The real problem came after her testimony before Congress. Since medical school, she'd studied, researched, and written about the inner workings of health insurance. Her research thesis for graduation with honors was based on real-world evidence of managed-care abuses. Ultimately, even though she hadn't sought attention, her writings were discovered. And though it wasn't woke to say it, it helped to be a svelte, photogenic, long-legged blonde with blue eyes and a gift for clarifying insurance jargon into everyday speech. Soon, she was giving lectures to advocate groups seeking better public health.

However, there was a flaw: public speaking frightened her. Small groups were OK, but a crowd—that unhinged her. As a featured dinner speaker, she found two or three glasses of chardonnay mellowed her out. Besides, she could tell the audience loved her.

After the interview on CNN and their special report on HMO abuses, her answering machine was jammed with more invitations. Her friends suggested a press agent. Both the *New York Times* and *Wall Street Journal* ran feature stories, and a literary agent even asked her to write a book titled *Managed Care Can Kill You.*

She knew that Andy was on the verge of proposing marriage. He always was. But in the social whirlwind, it was easy to dodge the question. Plus hook-ups were fun. It was a permanent honeymoon. For seven straight months, various civic groups wined and dined her. After each speech, she usually carried home an honorary award. Best of all, people were finally listening. It would have been impolite not to stay, socialize, and answer questions. How could she not have "just one more" glass?

She had worked hard for this recognition. She'd defeated Congressman Rye's efforts to remove regulations governing privately run medical laboratories. His attack dog, Malcolm Reinhardt, tried to humiliate her by portraying her as a disgruntled doctor simply pushing for higher fees. Yet it was Congressman Rye's legislation that had led to the death of his own wife. By facilitating the payment of Medicare dollars to cut-rate laboratories, of which he owned a chain, he unleashed shoddy medical care. As fate would have it, one of his labs misdiagnosed a tiny mole that later proved to be melanoma on his wife's back. She died six months later.

Susan's postgraduate thesis illuminated how overworked, undertrained lab technicians were pressured to increase volume over accuracy. The congressman used his lawyer to deflect the criticism. Publicly he depicted her as a millennial liberal. While Congressman Rye's TV ads showed a mature, sensible, and conservative advocate for better health care at lower cost, in the end, his greed and conflict of interest ensnared him. The House Committee on Ethics censured him, which forced his resignation.

For his part, Reinhardt claimed he was just a lawyer fulfilling his sworn oath to defend his client. As he said on the floor of Congress, "Truth shall prevail on the battlefield of justice."

But that battlefield had nearly killed her. So she earned her recognition for exposing the truth: managed care was a failed experiment. Alcohol simply squelched the jitters and shaped a clearer message. But soon she understood the words spoken to Julius Caesar when he'd led a tumultuous parade into a conquered city. Standing in the rear of Caesar's ornate chariot, a slave holding a golden crown whispered into his ear, "All fame is fleeting."

With time, her promised book deals and TV interviews vaporized. All that remained were the late-night parties and yet another chance to meet gentlemen who praised her talents and promised to spur her career. If she drank enough to believe their flattery, then the discussion adjourned to the hotel bedroom. But each morning, after she called her white knight, the reply message was a variation on "Great time, babe, but I'll need to get back to you on the other matter."

People warned her that book deals and movie rights were slow. They said, "Don't give up your day job."

Fortunately, her day job was booming. In fact, her medical practice had never been busier. Patients, like the elderly man with arthritis who nicknamed her the female Marcus Welby, wanted an honest doctor. Medicine was a great day job. But sometimes it became a night job. Like the night Lloyd Appleton bled. His gall bladder surgery had been routine. But that night, there were problems. She never drank before surgery, so he shouldn't have bled. The nurse called just as she was falling asleep with the guy who said he wrote scripts for Oprah Winfrey. The nurse made it sound serious.

"He doesn't look well. Doctor, I think you should come in."

The digits on the clock radio were blurred. They took shape to suggest 3:00 a.m. She thought about ordering another blood test or having the nurse watch Appleton and call back in an hour. Allow her head to clear. Yet another voice cried out, "A good doctor responds immediately." And as everyone said, she was a good doctor. Like the congressman from Iowa, who'd introduced her to the House of Representatives as "the role model for all good doctors."

In a raspy voice irritated by too much night-club smoke, she groaned, "I'll be right in."

She never expected that the nurse's estimate of bleeding was low. The flustered nurse was new and inexperienced. But this blood loss was serious.

In minutes, Appleton was on the operating table. Susan thought she could control it. But her ligature on the cystic artery had slipped off. That caused the artery to retract into the liver. As she tried to clamp it with a hemostat, the liver tore. It shouldn't have, but it did. He was too fat. He ate too much. It was difficult to see, and his liver was so damn cirrhotic. Besides, he smoked too much; what did he expect? Clamping deeper into the friable liver only made it bleed worse.

Afterward, they said the anesthesiologist had told her to transfuse more blood and to call for help, but she never remembered hearing that. She didn't hear anything until the anesthesiologist shouted, "Doctor, stop! You're drunk!"

Sometimes at night, his words haunted her. When Dr. Harrison entered the operating room, he stopped the bleeding, and she began to cry. Appleton's liver was shredded beyond repair. Three months later, in another hospital, he received a liver transplant. Two weeks later, she received a request for medical records.

That was when Malcolm Reinhardt had reappeared. On his first day in court, he bent over and whispered into her ear, "What goes around comes around."

On that same day, she also learned she couldn't "buck up" anymore. She desperately needed a drink. It kept the world back. It gave her space. But in that space, there was no room for Andy. After she lost the trial, which exceeded her insurance, the invitations, awards, and parties vanished. A drunken doctor and a defrocked priest: both are lonely people.

When her sister brought her to the airport on her way to Hazelden, Andy was there. She didn't want him there; she had told him a hundred times. But he came anyway to tell her, no matter how long, he would wait. Waving as she boarded the ramp, she saw he wore that silly ring on his left little finger. The same ring of friendship, one size too small, she'd given him so many years ago. He said he would wear it until she said yes. Now waiting outside the hospital conference room, she glanced at his left little finger. The ring was still there.

Chapter 9

When a young gentleman dressed in a gray vest and black suit opened the door, Susan and Andy were ushered into the conference room. John Friedman, as always, was at the table's head, while Drs. Harrison and Taylor were seated to his right. Drs. Joel Paulsen and Victor Starzack, from internal medicine, were seated across from them and appeared to be uncomfortable. As expected, Peter Regan was present and was busy shuffling a stack of legal papers. However, to Susan's surprise, seated next to Regan were Agent Monihan and Officer Stuhl. Without glancing at Andy, Susan could sense the hairs on the back of his neck bristle.

No sooner had they taken their seats, separated from the rest by a swath of open table, than CEO Freidman said, "I assume this is your attorney, Mr. Andrew Falcone?"

Andy nodded, and Freidman had everyone introduce themselves in round-table fashion. The young man who'd opened the door, and who was now seated on a small collapsible chair behind Freidman, typed frantically on his steno machine.

After introductions, Friedman said, "Gentlemen, I've asked Mr. Regan to chair this meeting to keep us on schedule. Dr. Whitney was invited to clarify the limits on her probationary license as dictated by the state department of health. This committee's job is to decide the future status of her hospital privileges."

As Peter Regan puffed out his chest, prepared to give a dissertation, he said, "We're not a court of law. The attorneys are present to assist their clients, and Special Task Force Investigator Jeffrey Stuhl is here at the request of the university president. Special Agent Jack Monihan from the FBI is present as part of his agency's investigation. And the physicians representing the hospital's credential committee are here as per hospital bylaws. They ensure quality medical care by reviewing the credentials and medical outcomes for qualified physicians."

Andy interjected, "Do all meetings of this committee have lawyers present, along with the FBI and university police?"

For several seconds, Regan's chest deflated. But after a deep breath, he said, "It depends on the individual case. What relevance does your question have?"

Calmly, Andy asked, "Then could you please furnish me with a list of previous committee meetings? And how many of those had lawyers, the FBI, and university police present? That might clarify the relevance of my question."

"Unfortunately, Mr. Falcone, meetings of this committee are privileged and not subject to disclosure, except to the state health department."

Raising his hand, Dr. Harrison, wearing blue surgical scrubs instead of a suit and tie, said, "If this is a meeting of doctors for doctors, how come it's only the lawyers who are talking?"

Friedman slashed him with a glare so severe, it should have left a scar. Then he snarled, "Attorney Regan is speaking on my behalf. Please don't interrupt him again."

As Harrison gazed down, it was clear he understood who buttered his bread.

Without skipping a beat, Regan continued, "Mr. Falcone, basically the credential committee feels that Dr. Whitney violated the conditions of her employment. Specifically, she should have used better judgment in caring for hospital patient Malcolm Reinhardt. That conclusion is based on expert medical opinions not appropriate for discussion here."

Andy's face flushed as he said, "If you've made your decision, why is my client here?"

"As stated in our letter, according to hospital bylaws, she has the opportunity to present additional information."

With a grimace, Andy barked, "Then we object to your process. Plus we demand specifics on how Dr. Whitney violated medical protocol in treatment of this or any patient."

Folding his hands on the table, Regan glared back. "It's the committee's opinion that she should have contacted her supervisors, as required by her temporary license."

Andy threw back, "What would another doctor have done differently? How was her treatment deficient?"

Dr. Taylor leaned forward, clearing his throat as though he had TB, and said, "Her judgment was poor. I was her supervisor that night. She didn't call me. Plus you wouldn't understand quality medical care. She used poor judgment."

As if he had been fouled, Andy threw his arm upward and gazed at Dr. Harrison as if he were a referee. "As chief of surgery, do you agree with that?"

As Susan's heart raced and her palms grew moist, she watched Harrison squirm. He glanced at Freidman and said, "She was in a hard spot. The patient survived, but she never called for help. The same issue she had years ago with another patient who bled after liver trauma."

Staring at Andy's face, she knew this wasn't the answer he'd expected. Dropping his arms, he shook his head and asked, "But shouldn't a doctor deal with the situation at hand and call for help as needed?"

Taylor interrupted again. "I was the one who got help. I mobilized the surgical team, arranged for necessary tests, and did all things that produce good, not shotgun, medical care."

Sensing the fatal blow had been delivered, Regan pronounced, "I believe you now see the committee's reasoning. Dr. Whitney violated her probation, and as such, her privileges should be revoked."

Andy pounded the table so hard his ring should have dented the wood. "I can assure you, gentlemen, we'll sue," he bellowed. "You've violated your bylaws and my client's right to a fair hearing."

Regan calmly stacked his papers and smirked. "Mr. Falcone, perhaps you shouldn't let your emotions cloud your judgment. Before you can sue this hospital, you'll need to appeal our decision to the New York State Public Health Council. Only if they find that we violated our bylaws and hospital procedure, can you take this case to court." Gathering his papers into a tight pile, he turned to face Freidman. "Is there anything further we should discuss?"

Hearing no response, and as if the room needed an additional kilowatt of electricity, Freidman said, "I've been asked by the university president and the chairman of the board of directors to allow Inspector Jeffrey Stuhl, the special task force investigator, to brief us."

Inspector Stuhl reached into the brown satchel lying next to him and extracted a manila folder of papers. Prolonging his moment in the spotlight, he slowly scanned the papers. Puckering his lips, he raised his head to stare at Susan and asked, "Can you tell us about this company you formed?"

Andy rose partially out of his chair. "By what right do you question my client?" he asked in a raised voice. "This is no longer a typical credential committee meeting."

Special Agent Monihan stared directly at Susan and said, "Doctor, Investigator Stuhl and I seek information on events surrounding the incident with Malcolm Reinhardt as well as information on your relationship with Dr. Raymond Dreskin. You may recall our first meeting—the meeting with you and plastic surgeon Dreskin?"

Inspector Stuhl, retaking the lead, continued, "Dr. Whitney, this meeting is being recorded, and you are free to ask us to leave. However, I must tell you that a federal grand jury has been impaneled. If you choose, we can subpoena your testimony. Dr. Dreskin has already been served."

As if she weren't there, Andy immediately responded, "I direct my client to not answer any of your questions, and we await your subpoena to my office."

Inspector Stuhl answered, "Fine. That's what we—"

Suddenly, Susan blurted out, "I'm not playing your games any longer. Spit out what you need to ask. I've nothing to hide."

Andy clutched her arm and leaned into her. "Sue, shut up. This is deadly serious. You could be sent to jail."

Flicking his hand away like a fly on a horse's tail, she glared at Stuhl. "My company, Spot of Hope, is a nonprofit 501(c) corporation. I formed it to help support physicians, dentists, nurses, and other medical workers struggling with drug or alcohol addiction. The company engages these same doctors and nurses to give back to their community during their own recovery by consoling and helping cancer patients cope with the complications of their illness."

In a tone that implied her company goals were similar to pedophilia, Stuhl asked, "So how much money do you take from this company?"

"I don't take any money. Each year it *costs* me money."

Stuhl opened the folder and tugged out what looked like a spreadsheet. "Certainly your company has expenses, such as handout materials for your lectures, coffee and doughnut costs for meetings, and rental of university rooms." He scanned the page. "Travel expenses and dinners to entertain wayward doctors?"

Andy stretched out his hand to touch her, but she reacted as though he were a burr beneath a saddle. Glaring back at Stuhl, she answered, "My expense reports are clearly documented and speak for themselves."

Stuhl tapped a folded-back page. "Yes, I see. But how about reimbursement to the university for use of their services and personnel?"

"I'm unclear as to what you mean."

"Well, of greater concern, your salary is partially supported by the university, correct?"

"Yes. I believe their contribution is $10,000 per year."

Stuhl then declared, "Since your efforts do little to enhance university goals, are you not guilty of theft of honest services?"

"Are you nuts or just a moronic, egotistical mall cop? I teach medical students and engage nurses in rehabilitation services for cancer patients. My work efforts support numerous university goals."

Andy stood up, glaring daggers at his client. Then, turning to face the group, he said, "Gentlemen, this meeting has ended."

Undeterred, Stuhl fixed his gaze on her. "Is that your request, Dr. Whitney?"

Before she could answer, Andy was already halfway out the door. Then Stuhl added, "And by the way, Doctor, can you explain the time mismatch between Dr. Dreskin's statement and yours on your whereabouts the morning of the attack on Mr. Reinhardt?"

With that, she stood and left the room.

Upon entering the corridor, she was surprised to see Andy a dozen paces ahead of her. As if prearranged, he stepped into an open elevator. By the time she arrived, the doors had closed.

Chapter 10

The following morning, ashamed to call Andy thanks to her outburst at the committee meeting, Susan craved a drink. She had already convinced herself that even the founder of Hazleton would agree. With trembling hands, she paced to the kitchen. The bottle of wine hidden beneath the sink, kept there as a symbol of her control, now called her. Pushing against her desire to drink, she returned to the bedroom and stared at the mirror above the bureau. If that image were a patient, she would have said, "You look terrible."

Analyzing her reflection, which resembled textbook pictures of young alcoholic women with sallow, wrinkled skin, her cravings dampened. As a surgeon, she knew that the organs beneath her skin were also decaying. But it was the ring of her phone that broke the morbid haze. Lifting it off the bureau, she identified Andy Falcone. Fearful of what to say, she whispered, "Hello."

In a weighty tone, he said, "Sue, I've just received your grand jury subpoena. I think you should see it as soon as possible."

As a flood of words filled her mind, she feared tripping over her words, so she simply asked, "May I come now?"

"I'm busy this morning, but I'll see you at one o'clock." Before she could answer, the connection went dead.

Unable to hold down more than a buttered bagel and two cups of coffee, she got ready and was in his waiting room at twelve thirty. Unlike physicians' offices, which were generally adorned with wall plaques, awards, degrees, licenses, and a coffee table heaped with pamphlets on good health, the walls of Andy's law office were bare except for an abstract painting that resembled a Rorschach blot. But what else, she concluded, other than pictures of drug dealers, would a federal defense lawyer hang up?

At 1:00 p.m. sharp, Andy's middle-aged assistant, wearing a black skirt and a gray long-sleeved blouse that matched the tinge of gray in her hair, opened the door and said, "Mr. Falcone will see you now."

Andy was seated at his desk, and she dropped into a red leather armchair across from him. The assistant scampered away without a word. Raising his gaze from the desktop, Andy opened fire. "Sue, we've known each other for many years. But don't ever do that to me again. You insulted me in public, which damaged my legal leverage and compromised your case." He paused to lift a thick document with an official blue backing. "Now your case is a serious criminal investigation."

As his glare burned, she answered, "I'm sorry, Andy. I was wrong. I lost it. But I never meant to hurt you."

Thrusting her subpoena across the desk, he said, "Here's your copy of the grand jury's demands. If you can abandon your superior attitude and shut up long enough to listen plus swear to never again pull such a go-it-alone stunt, I'll consider being your lawyer."

With a glare she had never seen before, he added, "But if you can't, I'll gladly refer you to several colleagues."

Having struggled with numerous misogynous surgeons, she knew how to hold her composure, but internally she longed to cry. She said, "Andy, I promise. You didn't deserve what I did. If you can forgive me and move past it, please be my lawyer." After a pause, she added, "And just know I'm scared to death."

Standing, he extended his hand. She rose and shook it with a smile, saying, "Although I don't know if I can afford you."

He suppressed his grin. "I know you can't, but let's get down to business." He lifted his copy of the subpoena. "These are the salient facts. I met with the assistant federal prosecutor this morning. Yesterday, over a dozen subpoenas were served. Besides yours, they were given to the hospital's attorney, Regan; CEO Freidman; Chief of Surgery Harrison; your supervisor, Dr. Taylor; and Dr. Dreskin as well as all the members of the credential committee and board of directors. And of course Malcolm Reinhardt and his sister, Grace."

Wide eyed, she exclaimed, "Why so many?"

"In the words of the infamous Sol Wachtler, chief justice of the court of appeals, 'A grand jury can indict a ham sandwich.'"

With a quizzical gaze, she asked, "What does that mean?"

"To obtain a true bill, the prosecutor will present to the grand jury as much one-sided evidence as possible. This may include unproven theories of guilt, lies, and even false testimony taken under oath."

Perceiving her confused expression, he added, "Basically, in order to indict you, the federal prosecutor needs to get a majority of the twenty-five jurists to agree with his interpretation that you committed a crime. If they do, it's called a true bill, and it authorizes indictment. Everyone who received a subpoena is expected to give information or evidence about the crime."

Gasping, she blurted, "What crime, and why me?"

"Let's back up a moment. This entire situation began with a complaint by someone who reported to law enforcement that they believed a crime was committed. More than likely, that complaint accuses you. Such an accusation triggers a police investigation, which is then reported to either a state or federal prosecutor. The prosecutor's office gathers more evidence and testimony to determine the validity of the original complaint. If that investigation supports the prosecutor's opinion that he could successfully convict you in a jury trial, then he will ask the grand jury to indict you. Everyone called in front of the grand jury is either a witness against you or a target alongside you."

"What am I, target or witness?" she asked, realizing it was a rhetorical question.

"Sue, both you and Dr. Dreskin are targets. Everyone called so far, and perhaps more to come, is a witness against you and Dreskin."

"What the hell are they accusing me of?"

"Their accusations are many. For example, against that company of yours, which I know nothing about, they claim wire fraud, theft of honest services, misuse of federal funds, and embezzlement."

Aghast, she said, "What the hell are they talking about?"

"Sue, we'll be spending weeks going into those particulars. But they don't end there. The more serious accusations are based on your animus toward former congressman Rye and his surrogate, Malcolm Reinhardt. The investigators are stretching those charges into a hate crime to go along with the charges of first-degree assault and torture. Whoever is behind this effort to get you is so obsessed they're even trying to discover new legal precedent with their charge of torture."

Waving her subpoena, she said, "Look. The first line of this thing commands me to appear before the grand jury next week. So let's go and end this thing. This is goddamn ridiculous."

He hung his head. "This is exactly what you promised a minute ago not to do." After a pause, he gazed at her and said, "Now listen. First off, our goal is to avoid having you appear before the grand jury. Especially considering your volatile temper." He thumped his desktop. "Let me educate you on the system. If you go before the grand jury, I can't go inside the grand jury room. You would be alone. No opportunity to talk to me. Zero chance for any legal help. Anything you say, no matter how unintended, would be used against you at trial. The prosecutor and lead investigators would keep you there and grill you. And in your case, God only knows what you would say before you explode." Shaking his head, he added, "Sue, if a grand jury can indict a ham sandwich, I'm confident you could leave that room indicted for assassinating Lincoln."

Although it was no joking matter, she smiled and dropped the subpoena on the desk. "Sometimes I'm an ass, but I'm never ungrateful. I'm sorry, Andy. Please tell me what to expect, and I'll shut up."

After a long sigh, he folded his hands and answered, "I know all of this is new and complex. The legal pressures you'll face could destroy you. I once had a client, a doctor, who was viciously investigated, like I'm certain you will be. After three years of relentless, unmerciful innuendoes, the FBI dropped his case. But the investigation destroyed his reputation, life's work, and past triumphs. In addition, the prolonged stress lowered his immune system, which triggered two rare, incurable cancers. After major surgical, medical, and radiation treatment, plus all their complications, he's still under biweekly chemotherapy and remains a shell of his former self."

Taking another deep breath, he continued, "You ask what comes next. I'll tell you everything—not to frighten you but to prepare you. Like most Americans, you believe you're innocent until proven guilty. Technically, that's true, but it's not. In order to survive this battle, you'll need to respond to the demands within this twenty-two-page subpoena. That'll take several months, perhaps a year or more. You'll need to gather documents, emails, bank statements, invoices, payments, witness statements, and other things to defend every action you took over the past several years. All this information will require organization and conversion into specific legal formats. The lead investigator will likely request more material. The cost of these paralegal services will likely exceed $50,000, which I can't pay for you."

On the edge of losing her stamina, she gasped, "Years?"

"Sue, have you ever heard the expression, 'Don't make a federal case out of it'? That means don't drag it out. But federal cases are structured to drag it out."

"Why?"

"So the prosecutor can force a settlement. Make a target plead guilty to a felony or else risk a longer prison sentence should they choose a trial. That plea deal fortifies society's belief that justice is served. It verifies the untarnished faith that the FBI always gets its man. Plus there's the public's belief that the bureau wouldn't accuse an innocent person. Where there's smoke, there's fire."

"But I did nothing wrong."

He took another deep breath. "You've told me several times you're innocent. Your premise is that innocent people don't go to jail. But federal investigations cripple a person's mind. Their reputations are besmirched, they're fired, future dreams evaporate, and yes, many go to jail. Why? Because people break down. They can't afford the emotional burden, the cost, the fact that most if not all their friends have left them. Seeing yourself in front-page print or on the TV news or being first in a Google search is never a career enhancer. So given enough time, pressure, and debt, people plead guilty to whatever felony is offered."

"Yeah, but I won't do that."

"Good. You'll need that courage and stamina to survive."

As she slumped deeper into the chair, he said, "Let's postpone more details. Take the subpoena home, gather your thoughts, and let's meet again."

Too weak to stand, she asked, "What's this thing with Dr. Dreskin? And who is the lead investigator?"

Andy rose slowly and began to pace back and forth in front of the large window behind his desk. After rubbing his forehead, he said, "I'm not sure how to answer that. Several facts confuse me. Evidently Dreskin appears to have almost as much animus for Malcolm Reinhardt as you do. Some woman, his patient, is suing him over a bad face-lift. And Malcolm Reinhardt was her malpractice lawyer. I think the woman has been served or will be soon."

Retaking his seat, Andy flipped pages and said, "Most unusual is the fact that the lead investigator for this case is Inspector Jeffrey Stuhl."

Startled, she said, "He's a university cop—one step lower than a mall cop."

He nodded. "There we have agreement. I've had past cases dealing with him and the university. He's a pompous, self-righteous, pontificating bastard who's a legend in his own mind."

Sue interjected, "What the hell does he have to do with the FBI?" She threw up her arms. "And what's this bullshit card he hands out with the title 'FBI task force officer'? Is he a lawyer or an accountant? I thought those were the requirements to be a special agent."

Shaking his head, he answered, "Again, dealing with reality, he loves titles that glorify him. But in cases that involve the university, Stuhl is their man. He supposedly had a police job at the Capitol in Washington before coming to the university. And he's one compulsive investigator that follows the money and his gut feelings." He sighed. "Unfortunately, overworked FBI agents fighting terrorism, drugs, and high crimes need to depend on task forces to offload some work. Judging by his questions yesterday, Stuhl is clearly focused on your company thing. And it explains why the federal prosecutor this morning stated they're investigating you for wire fraud, theft of university service, and embezzlement."

Standing, he said, "Look, Sue, we can't do more today. Let me do my job, and let's meet another day."

As he walked past her, Susan still slumped in her chair and folding her subpoena into her purse, he said, "My assistant will set up another appointment."

When she gazed upward, he was gone. In the whirlwind of facts, she felt like the ancient mariner in Samuel Coleridge's poem: "He went like one that hath been stunned, / And is of sense forlorn: / A sadder and a wiser man, / He rose the morrow morn."

Chapter 11

Seated on her green sofa, staring at a photograph on the fireplace mantel, Cindy yearned to recapture the feelings she had when she was runner-up in the Miss New York beauty pageant. Grasping the portable phone next to her, she squeezed it so hard the plastic groaned. As her gaze shifted to an adjacent photograph, she floundered in the memories of working as a congressional intern for Congressman Rye. She had met so many important people. She was clearly on the path to becoming someone. But now, except for her one dear friend, who always stood by her, she was a forgotten runner-up, never a queen.

The miniature clock on the end table chimed two bells. As the sound echoed in her ears, she felt her skin crawl and her heart race. Holding up the phone, she saw its face lit up as she said, "Two a.m., Attorney Peller, time to wake up."

With a tremulous finger, she tapped out his number and said, "Wouldn't it have been easier to just serve him with papers?"

Bringing the phone to her ear gingerly, so as not to disturb the snake, she listened for the ring. By the second ring, she expected to hear his drowsy voice, but instead a woman screamed, "Stop it! Stop calling!"

Holding her breath, she squeezed the phone harder and listened for the sound of fear. Mustering her inner power, she tried to see right through the phone. See inside their bedroom. She hoped they were squirming, just like the snake. She wondered what his wife looked like. That harlot, who enjoyed the benefits of his high fees. She was probably pretty and certainly without scars.

And from the sound of her voice, she was young, younger than he was, that bastard.

Again the woman shouted, "Stop calling here! The police know who you are."

She almost gasped but didn't. The police couldn't possibly know for sure. Patience. Make them wonder. Steady. Maintain the pressure.

Just as the woman was hanging up, Cindy, thanks to her powers of concentration, heard the harlot say, "I can't stand—"

And then the line went dead. Still clutching the phone, Cindy said aloud, "Oh, yes, you can. You can stand a whole lot more."

Ending the call, she placed the phone on her lap and leaned against the pillow. The ticking clock now was so loud that she held her palms over her ears. As the ticking grew louder, she pressed harder, taking the chance it might anger the snake. But she must wait. Wait until the clock chimed three. Ever so slowly the ticking faded, and then she closed her eyes.

When the phone rang, at first, she thought it was a dream. It rang again. Patting her lap, she found it wasn't there. It must have rolled off the couch. Spotting the green flash on the floor, she picked it up and said, "Hello."

There was nothing but silence. She said even louder, "Hello…hello… who's there?"

Then a mechanical voice said, "You bitch, you fucking ugly bitch. Why don't you kill yourself?"

The line went dead. The air in the room was silent. Even the ticking clock seemed dead. Staring at the phone, she saw the screen display "unknown name, unknown number," and she screamed, "God help me—please."

Chapter 12

Seated on the couch, four steps from the wall with a TV, which for Malcolm functioned as a radio, he turned to face the warmth from the gas fireplace to his left. It provided scant heat, but it crackled as though real wood were burning. Awaiting Grace's arrival, he mulled over his bleak future. Ever since his discharge from the hospital, his afflictions weighed heavily on him. Seated alone, at fifty-one years of age, he felt more plant than animal. He would never again be a vibrant man. Muttering aloud, he said, "Is this how my life ends, rotting in an old folks' home?"

When he was ten, his parents had decided it was time to place Grandma in an old folks' home, which was what these buildings were called back then. Etched in his mind was the day they'd brought her there. As they drove away, he stared out the car's rear window as Grandma shrunk to the size of a doll. He thought she was smiling and waving, but perhaps it wasn't a smile, and might she actually have been waving at them to come back? For the next two years, they only saw her every other Sunday.

In today's politically correct society, these structures were no longer called old folks' homes but rather long-term care facilities. Though the name sounded much better, he knew they still remained storage containers for people scheduled to die.

While driving to work each morning, he passed such a place. A two-story building that was formerly a motel with forty-eight rooms. Before it became a long-term care facility, it was a short-term fun facility known for afternoon delights. Originally scheduled for demolition, the building gained a new life when the owner, a man with political connections and a hunger for Medicaid dollars, cashed in his political favors to secure a certificate of need from the state. And presto, the building became a nursing home.

On his way to work each morning, if he caught the corner's red traffic light, he would stare at the gray-haired people through the building's large front window. Like mannequins with fixed expressions, the residents were seated around square tables. He rarely saw them eat; instead they only gawked at their feet. Even if he caught a long red light, he never saw any of the residents move, and he wondered when they ate.

Good manners dictated he should avert his stare, but their mismatched clothes and gaping mouths that suggested dribbling saliva only made him vow to never grow old. Yet some of the people weren't old. Like the two young men in wheelchairs with limbs twisted by palsy. On some days, it appeared as if they were waving, but he couldn't be certain it wasn't spasms.

When the light turned green, he would hit the gas, which drove their image out of his mind. Such thoughts could paralyze a man peaking in his career. Yet now here he was, one of them. Turning his head as if he could see, he wondered if he ate behind such a picture window. Grace assured him that this facility was outstanding. She called it a suite. For the price he paid, it should be. She told him his room was on the top floor, a corner apartment with two large windows, a fireplace, and more. At least motorists couldn't see this high.

His nurse, a kind middle-aged lady, had just left the room after bringing him fresh towels. Hearing the door close, he couldn't help but fear someone else was there. Scanning the room as if his eye sockets had sensors, he searched for Grace. The policeman who'd formerly stood outside his hospital door now was gone. Instead, the lieutenant had assured him, "We'll have a patrol car keep an eye on the place."

How good was that, being guarded by the same police who still hadn't made an arrest? The ATF was still investigating the suspicious fire and had concluded thus far that it must have been a loose wire in a faulty light switch. Although, they emphasized, with so much gas, a spark from his shoe would have done the job.

If he had been home, as Jane wanted, perhaps things would have been different. Since robbery wasn't a motive in the explosion, Inspector Stuhl concluded it was a grudge. So far, Stuhl was focused on only two suspects, although Malcolm was repeatedly asked about anyone who might have reason to harm him. But his memory was still vague. The images from that night were incomplete. And the snapshots he recalled he would only share with Grace. So for Inspector Stuhl's benefit, he tried to remember dissatisfied clients.

Most of his clients were upset with their settlements. The nastiest were unemployed litigants who viewed suing a doctor as a job opportunity. But contrary to what he claimed in his ads, which boasted million-dollar awards, victory in malpractice was rare and risky. Less than 15 percent of cases ended in the client's favor. With odds of losing more than four out of five, his firm chose clients wisely. Weak claims were settled out of court, generally for around $50,000. After subtracting his third, plus costs for his paralegals and expert witnesses, the injured patient was lucky to pocket five grand. This left some litigants bitter, and they unleashed nasty letters or phone calls. Some used Facebook, but his paid advertising overwhelmed their paltry, misspelled complaints.

Hearing the doorknob rattle, he felt his heart race. It should be Grace, but until he heard her voice, he held his breath. And he wondered when this anxiety would leave him.

Whoever it was closed the door and snapped the lock. Then he heard Grace say, "Great news. They just fired Whitney." After she fumbled with hangers in the closet, he heard the reclining mechanism of the leather chair clunk. "Isn't that great? Plus I've got a ton of things to tell you."

"I have some things on my mind also."

"I had some colleagues dig around the prosecutor's office. They're pretty confident that Whitney had an accomplice in her attack on you. Maybe it's Dr. Dreskin, although they believe he's not bright enough to do it alone." After a pause, she added, "Of course, our best dog in the hunt is Inspector Stuhl. Thank God the FBI and the prosecutor have given him free reign."

"Grace, I agree. And I need to tell you something."

"Of course, anything. Is your memory clearing?"

Shifting in his chair, he said, "Yes. And it worries me."

"Why?" she asked.

"Remember when I said it had something to do with when I stumbled over her body? Well, now I'm certain I saw blood. Blood all over my hand after I touched her. Blood on the floor. At that moment, I couldn't see it clearly. But I saw a dark contrast across my hand. And it felt sticky."

Touching his hand, she said, "You'll remember everything in time. We just need to concentrate. Stay focused on what's critical to our case."

"It was when I knelt down," he said.

"What?"

"I knelt down to roll her over." He cleared his throat. "Now those thoughts are an obsession. Thoughts I need to verify. If there was blood on the floor, is it possible some of it stuck to my clothes?"

Hearing her slide off the recliner, he knew she was standing as she answered, "Well, I know how to solve this. When you were discharged from the hospital, they gave me a bag containing your clothes. It was a bit gruesome, so I threw the bag in one of your closets. Let me go look."

Hearing her high heels clatter across the wooden floor, he wondered what she would find. After what seemed like an eternity, she returned and said, "We'll need to get a lab analysis, but the pants are odd."

Sighing deeply, he said, "What do you see?"

"Both legs of the pants were cut on their inner side, probably as they searched for a leg vein to start an IV. However, the right leg is suspicious. On the outside surface where the knee would be, there's a dark brownish oval stain. But it's badly charred. However, on the inside of that same pant, in the same place, there's an oval area stained a darker red. As if something soaked through. It does looks like old blood."

He gasped. "My God, Grace, she was bleeding before I found her!" Trying to slow his heart, he added, "We need to get this to the police for proper analysis and to confirm DNA."

"Wait, Malcolm. You're still confused. Think for a moment. How could Whitney or even Dreskin get into the house? Jane knew what Whitney looks like. She hated her, perhaps even more than you do. Could it have been Dreskin? Perhaps. But he's a stranger, and I doubt Jane would have let him in. Could it have been a hired killer that muscled his way inside? That's a possibility."

He was shaking now. "I'm not sure I follow you. Spell it out."

"If Jane let someone into the house, someone who ultimately killed her, she must have known him or at least trusted him. Plus keep in mind Whitney was working in the hospital on a twenty-four-hour shift that day."

"I think I see where you're going."

Hearing a leather skirt slide across the leather recliner, he knew she was seated as she said, "I told you there's more I need to tell you. Last night, I had a secret dinner meeting with the chairman of the hospital board of directors, along with his vice-chair. It actually was at the chairman's home. Throughout the dinner, they danced around the subject. But I finally got them to the point. Basically, here's their problem: they're afraid that our litigation will devastate their annual financial report. But here's the kicker—they want this to end in order to kill the publicity. They have a major application in process to become an NCI-designated comprehensive cancer center. I mean a real major center just south of here in the center of New York state in the Finger Lakes region."

He interrupted, saying, "I've heard rumors to that effect."

Unfazed, she continued, "Plus the three major medical universities are threatening to pull out should they fail. They informed me of the fact that of the fifteen hundred cancer centers in the US, only fifty-one are officially approved by the National Cancer Institute as comprehensive cancer centers. New York state already has four—three in New York City and one in Roswell Park in Buffalo. But these boys want to lock up the central zone of the state because of the massive land available and because the central location would pull patients from overcrowded New York City, Canada, and states south."

All he could add was, "Wow."

"Malcolm, can you imagine the money this means? Are we going to let that Whitney bitch stand in our way? The men last night offered to triple our wildest lawsuit settlement, which of course will never be made public. All they want from us is to support their story that Whitney is a rogue doctor who never was a full-time employee. They had no way of knowing she was a liar and a vengeful felon." She snickered, "Of course we'll take the triple payout and a whole lot more."

Grasping his scarred right hand, she said, "Look, not to put too fine a point on it, you were publicly hurt by that bitch. You deserve compensation. You feel guilty about Jane's death. But let's face it—she was very sick and bound to die. Plus I know how unhappy your marriage was for the past several years. What's past is gone. We need to focus on you. With more time to heal, you can someday be an active lawyer again. Your mind is still great. You could dictate your responses to paralegals who read their case summaries to you."

After a long pause, he said, "Those trousers are exculpatory evidence. Didn't we take an oath that obligates us to turn them in? They're significant in finding the real killer."

"Malcolm, the only oath I know is family first."

"But what do we do now? How would we cover our tracks?"

He heard her stand and walk past him, and then the sound of the fireplace grew louder. In seconds, the odor of burning cloth filled the room, and he coughed.

Then she said, "I just took care of our problem."

Chapter 13

As Cindy sat in her parked car across the street from Peller's apartment, she hugged the silver package. Stealing his identity had been easy. But masquerading as his secretary, Joyce, and calling the building manager to convince him that her boss had lost his key and needed another before tonight's gala event—that was far more difficult. Thank goodness for her acting lessons. She also pled with the manager to contact the locksmith and arrange for her to pick up the key. Apologizing profusely for the inconvenience, she assured him that Mr. Peller would be extra generous over the holidays. After a call to the locksmith and paying with Peller's Mastercard, Cindy got the key that afternoon.

Glancing at the folded newspaper lying on the car seat, she studied Amy Peller's picture. She looked radiant. Certainly she didn't need a scarf to hide her face. The caption beneath her photo noted she was the chairwoman for tonight's event, which benefited the American Cancer Society. How phony they were. What did they care about cancer? Their only goal was free publicity. Scratching the picture with a long red fingernail, she shredded the face.

Suddenly, a silver limousine double-parked in front of their apartment. It had to be for them. Squinting at the tinted car windows, she spied silhouettes moving. As the heads leaned back, it appeared they were laughing and enjoying a glass of wine. They were having fun, something she would never have again.

Then, at the top of the stone staircase, Mike Peller appeared. He was dressed in a white tuxedo. His red cummerbund accented his wife's strapless pink dress. Dashing gallantly ahead, he opened the limo's door, stood like a soldier, and waved his arm to sweep her in. With a laugh heard down the block, he jumped in behind her, and the car sped away.

She waited several minutes before carefully tightening her scarf and opening her door. Using two hands, she gingerly lifted the package. Striding toward his building, she thought about how long it had taken to find just the right gift. At the front door, she set the box down and smiled as her key unlocked the entrance. Inside the foyer, she saw the elevators down the hall. Hugging the box to her chest, she pressed the up button and, once inside, the eleventh-floor button.

Her key unlocked the door labeled 1102 as she hoped. Immediately entering the living room, she extracted a small flashlight from her trench coat and swept the floor. Normally, she would have admired the oriental rug and the embroidered sofa, but she was there to work. Spotting the far hallway, she strode toward it. Both walls were covered with family photos of the Pellers as children. How quaint, she thought. She entered the master bedroom, where the scent of perfume soaked the air. The king-sized rice bed had four carved corner posts that nearly touched the ceiling. The partially opened drawer of the heavy armoire had a scarf draping over its edge. Sweeping the light over it, Cindy saw the pure red color of quality silk shimmer back. A wrinkled navy blue cocktail dress, twisted on a hanger, was tossed across the bed. She must have discarded it for something better, Cindy thought, just like they did with people. Try them, use them, and then dispose of them.

The bathroom light, which they had left on, cast long shadows. Entering the spacious boudoir, she detected the scent of lavender lingering in the warm damp air. On the vanity counter, an open mascara bottle, blue eye shadow, and a tube of Colgate with a missing cap had all been abandoned. Staring at the dribble of toothpaste, she thought, Someone must have been in a hurry.

Two bath towels were crumpled on the floor next to the spacious glass shower. Droplets of water had streaked down the side and coalesced as if they could avoid evaporation. Turning toward the vanity counter, she cautiously placed the silver box on it. The row of lights around the mirror were so bright they easily could have pierced her scarf and frightened the snake. Carefully averting her gaze, she focused on the metal box. Gently rubbing it, she felt its coolness. She squeezed it ever so softly. It seemed peaceful inside. Of course, that would only last until she opened the bottle.

Pocketing the flashlight, she backed away. Then, reaching into her other pocket, she pulled out the small brown bottle with the rubber bulb top. Holding it at arm's length as if it were plutonium, she scanned the room. The pile of towels on the floor would do just fine. Squatting down, she used two fingers and fashioned a cave among folds in one of the towels. Then, squeezing the rubber bulb, she slowly unscrewed the top. She lifted the plastic dropper, making certain that its tip remained inside the bottle. Waiting several seconds until no droplets fell, she lifted it free. Taking care not to touch her clothes, she held the dropper over the towel's cave. She squeezed the bulb hard, and a steady stream of clear fluid streaked out. She replaced the dropper, screwed it tight, and stared at the box. It was quiet.

When she was a teenager, her father had warned her about this catastrophic mixture. Once the pheromones hit the air, no power on earth could deter the soldiers. Racing back to the bedroom, she lifted the cover over two pillows. With the same care she had used in the bathroom, she squirted a dropperful beneath each pillow. With the bottle safely in her pocket, she darted back to the bathroom.

Placing a fist on the box lid, she unsnapped the clasp and held her breath. The sudden vibration alarmed the inhabitants. A steady buzz filled her ears. Hopefully it wouldn't scare the snake. Pressing harder on the lid with her fist, she scanned the room one more time. Then, mentally retracing her exit, she pulled out the flashlight and turned it on. She used the flashlight as a tool to open the cover. For one split second, she gazed into the cauldron of swarming bees as they crawled over each other. But all she really saw were stingers protruding from swollen striped bodies. Several were already crawling over the sides as they danced in orgasmic fantasy, anticipating their fertile queen.

Before the buzzing exploded in her ears, she streaked from the bathroom and raced for the front door. Locking it behind her, she scanned the corridor and congratulated herself on her luck: the corridor was empty. Pocketing the flashlight, she tightened her scarf and strode for the elevator. She glanced back, envisioning the frustrated bees as they searched for their queen. When the elevator opened, she wondered if Michael, like the bees, might have romance on his mind tonight.

When the door closed, she hoped for his sake that he hadn't drunk too much wine.

Chapter 14

The next morning, Grace burst into Malcolm's apartment and shrieked, "Goddamn it to hell, Mike and Amy are in the hospital! It's out of control!"

As she slammed the door and snapped the dead bolt, he heard her heels thump on the wooden floor and then become muffled as she dashed into his carpeted bedroom. Bolted awake by his racing heart, but afraid to interrupt, he concentrated on sensing the draft from her frantic pacing.

Suddenly, she stopped and howled, "Who's doing this?"

"For God's sake, what happened?"

"Last night, Mike and Amy were attacked by bees, hundreds of them. They're in the hospital in serious condition. They were killer bees. A goddamn special strain of them."

"Oh my God!"

"Luckily the neighbors heard screams and called police. Amy was passed out in the corridor, covered with them. The firemen sprayed her with foam."

Now fully awake and sitting on the edge of his bed, he asked, "Then what?"

"Took the firemen over an hour to rescue them. All the while Mike was screaming, firemen evacuated the floor. What cruel bastard did this?"

Rubbing his hands over his corrugated face, he couldn't help but appreciate his bark-like skin. Thumping a thick scar on his forehead, he knew no bee had a stinger long enough to pierce it. Then he said, "What do the cops say?"

"I called Stuhl and demanded he come to your apartment to meet with us. He should be here any minute."

It was interesting how she called his place an apartment. If this was an apartment, it was a strange one. An apartment where they made him eat alone. But he knew the truth. He could tell by the flurry of footsteps when the young aides brought his food. They were repulsed. His isolation was intended to make him feel special. But even his neighbor, the old man with Alzheimer's, wasn't allowed to see him.

The knock on the door broke his thoughts. Next, he heard Grace's icy-cold greeting. "Inspector Stuhl, please come in and sit down."

Grace returned to the bedroom and guided him into the living area. Malcolm heard Stuhl say, "Mr. Reinhardt, how are you, sir?"

Plunging his hands beneath the blanket on his lap, he answered, "Not well, Inspector. But more importantly, will all my partners need to be attacked before you make an arrest?"

"No, sir, but I do have some questions. May I sit down?"

At least Stuhl had asked before sitting down, Malcolm thought; that showed some respect. "Sure, please do," he said. But of course he couldn't verify if Stuhl had waited for his reply.

Grace initiated the cross-examination. "What kind of maniac did this? Use *bees*, for God's sake. Do you have any clues? What about our friend Whitney? She's never off my list."

Matching her decibels, Stuhl interrupted, "Ma'am, we're working on multiple leads. I assure you all suspects have our attention." Lowering his voice, he continued, "As you know, Amy Peller sustained fewer bee stings than her husband. She's regained consciousness, and I spoke to her. She told me about the harassing phone calls. Are you aware of those?"

After a long pause, Grace said, "No…not at all. Malcolm, you know anything?"

"No. Mike never mentioned anything like that. He's called to see how I was doing, but we never talked shop."

"We checked his phone records and discovered late-night calls from a Ms. Cynthia Franklin. Does that name ring a bell?"

Hearing her name triggered an explosion, and Malcolm said, "Yes. I know her. Mike must have picked up her case."

"Yes, he did," Stuhl answered. "Public records show it's a malpractice case against a Dr. Raymond Dreskin."

"That's correct. She's a very disturbed woman, obsessed with her surgeon."

"Mr. Reinhardt, did she have a grudge against you?"

"Why ask him, for Christ's sake?" Grace screeched. "Haul her ass in and ask her."

"Ma'am, I know you're upset. However, there are procedures. As an attorney, I'm sure you understand civil rights." With less sarcasm, he said, "We've spoken with Dr. Dreskin previously. He reported receiving late-night calls, which he ascribed to Ms. Franklin."

Grace snapped back, "Well, there you have it."

Stuhl cleared his throat. "But there's a problem. The doctor won't help us. It appears you've sued him several times in the past. Anyway, due to his problems with you, he's not sympathetic to helping you."

"Oh, goddamn..." Grace said.

Unwavering, Stuhl continued, "Actually the doctor blames you, Mr. Reinhardt. He feels the woman is a mental case that you encouraged by undertaking her lawsuit."

On the verge of losing her courtroom decorum, Grace howled, "Well, screw him and the entire medical profession for committing malpractice. Look at my brother. Look at him! Now this sniveling prima donna refuses to help. Did he ask you to lower the cap payment on malpractice too?"

He heard Stuhl's feet shuffle and then felt a hand on his knee. "Mr. Reinhardt, did this woman ever make any threats to you?"

He hesitated. "I don't recall, but she was overanxious that we settle her case."

"That's all I need. Thank you, sir."

Hearing several footsteps, Malcolm then heard Stuhl say, "Ma'am, thank you also. We'll be in touch."

In a tone normally reserved for witnesses she hadn't yet excused, she said, "Detective, what are you planning to do about her? And is she connected to Whitney?"

"Ma'am, we're looking into every lead. Good day."

Snapping the dead bolt after him, she said, "These cops are useless. We need to do something ourselves."

"I agree, Grace. This Franklin woman is a basket case. Cripes, she couldn't sit still for thirty seconds. She's too insane to orchestrate all this, but she could screw up our goal on Whitney and the hospital deal. I think Whitney is using her as a tool."

He crunched his fingers until the numbness was replaced with pain, then said, "Perhaps it's time to hire our own detectives."

He heard her sit and stifle a laugh. "That's an excellent idea. I'll call my California office. There are a couple ex–LA detectives I use for such purposes. Let's just say we do things differently out west."

And for the first time in a long time, he leaned back and opened his mouth wider than ever before, stretching the scars until he could no longer stand the pain. Only then did he join her in a laugh.

Chapter 15

On the nameplate, beneath W. Harrison MD, a second label read Chief of Surgery. Susan wondered how many people knew that the W stood for Worthington. Even fewer, she bet, knew that after his family name, the Roman numeral III should be printed. Though she had visited his office many times, no visit had ever required a trench coat with a pulled-up collar and a dark bonnet beneath a baseball cap pulled down to nearly cover her eyes. However, since her hospital dismissal, prudence demanded she avoid recognition. Fortunately, the morning's weather provided an excuse for both the coat and head covering.

Slipping into his assistant's office, she removed her gear as Linda said, "Dr. Whitney, that's some outfit. Your grandmother's?"

Laughing, she said, "Thanks. Actually, it's a holdover from my days with the CIA."

Leaving her desk, Linda hugged her tightly and said, "How've you been, dear?" Then she gasped. "My Lord, have you lost weight? Let me get you something really quick."

"No, thanks, I'm fine. Is the boss in?"

"He sure is. Been waiting for you." With a wink, she added, "I canceled his other appointment, so take your time."

Her knock triggered his booming voice. "Come in."

Entering the office, she wondered how he managed to pile so many magazines on a single desk. Medical journals, opened textbooks, and photocopied articles were all stacked into teetering towers. And as always Dr. Harrison was dressed in what medical students swore was his only suit: blue surgical scrubs.

The perfect gentleman from yesteryear, he leaped to his feet and said, "Sue, good to see you. Here, sit. Let me move these journals."

Grabbing a pile off the worn, overstuffed chair, she answered, "It's OK, Dr. Harrison. I've got them." Scanning where to drop them, she concluded he had already memorized them, and she placed them on the floor next to her. She sank into the soft chair. "I'm not here to push you onto a limb. I just need your advice."

"You know I can't be pushed onto a limb. Now tell me—what's on your mind?"

Sighing, she continued, "As you know, after firing me, the hospital filed to lift my license. Plus the police believe I tortured Reinhardt. In addition, they're trying to pin his wife's murder on me. Then there are the charges that I embezzled from the university with my company, Spot of Hope. So where do I have a friend?"

Leaning back in his chair, he dropped his gaze, which she knew was his way of collecting his thoughts. It gave her time to recall how much she owed this man. As her professor, teacher, mentor, and most importantly her friend, he'd wisely guided her throughout her rising career. Over the five long years of surgical residency, where she'd been one of only three females, she couldn't recall the number of times she wanted to quit. Become a dermatologist, her fellow residents derided. Yet Dr. Harrison had always convinced her to tear up her letter of resignation.

Taking a deep breath, she said, "I don't know what to do anymore. I just can't catch a break. I attend AA meetings every day and take my daily challenges one at a time. I no longer have high expectations, and I try to focus on things I can do. But I'm sinking deeper each day. I can't figure out why Taylor hung me out to dry that morning in Friedman's office. He used to be a doctor with high moral standards. Now he's become a greedy company man." Feeling a push of tears behind her eyes, she turned her head away.

As always, he spoke in the nick of time. "Sue, let's analyze this one step at a time."

Blinking as if her lids were squeegees, she answered, "Where do we start?"

"Sue, why do think the they're blaming you for Reinhardt's attack?"

"First, they figure it must be someone with knowledge of hospital routine.

And it's easy to say I had motive. Finally, I was in the hospital during the attack."

Raising an eyebrow, he asked, "You were here? Didn't you go home after our meeting?"

Shifting in her chair, she said, "No; I was in the cafeteria, feeling sorry for myself. Anyway, that university cop, an FBI agent, and Friedman came in, saw me, and started asking questions. Friedman didn't help by grilling me as to why I hadn't left the hospital. Ray Dreskin got them off me when he popped out and told them I was with him all morning."

"Was he?"

"No. Not all morning, just part of it. I don't recall how long. But he told them all morning."

"Why he'd do that?"

"He said afterward that he couldn't stand watching the hospital screw with me."

Leaning back, Harrison said, "Well, maybe that cosmetic surgeon has some backbone after all. Not much, but some."

"So anyway, that's where I stand, a felon without a license."

Gazing into her eyes, he said, "Sue, things aren't always what they seem. I shouldn't have to tell you, a surgeon." As if he could stare into her soul, he paused to let the last word sink in. "A few years ago, you tackled a tiger. I don't mean the crooked congressman but rather the medical insurance industry."

"What do you mean?"

"Remember the Oliver Stone movie about Nixon? How the military-industrial complex drove America's economy? Well, the medical insurance industry is very similar."

As his eyes sparkled, she knew he was planning a lecture. A confidence builder, like the ones he would give her so many years ago.

This one began, "By now everyone knows managed medical care is a failed experiment. Medical insurance premiums haven't dropped one cent. They've increased by double digits every year. Hell, the other day, I read the CEO of Starbucks claims he spends more on health insurance than he does on coffee beans." He tapped a pile of journals on his desk. "You, my dear, have pissed them off. They never forgot, or forgave, the thrashing you gave them on national news. You spotlighted their flaws. You stripped away their cloak of false compassion and illuminated their bottom-line greed for profit. You tampered with multimillion-dollar salaries for CEOs, hospital executives, and university executive vice presidents for health affairs, not to mention signing bonuses and golden parachutes."

As she listened, she recalled her past dinner speeches. It was like he had written them. But now she realized that when she'd drunk more than two glasses of chardonnay and laced every other sentence with a personal diatribe about an overpaid CEO, she'd only received a fizzle of applauses.

As if her mentor could read her mind, he paused and said, "Of course, it's not only businessmen who profited. The medical profession has its own share of entrepreneurs."

"You mean like Taylor?"

"How did you get his shorts in such a knot?"

She shrugged. "I can't stand the asshole."

"None of us can. But he's a great example of doctors turning from medical practice to hospital and insurance administration. The board of directors loves him. He tells them exactly what they want to hear. He applauds decisions they've already made. He promises to bring those pesky doctors in line. Get them to understand the challenges of the business community, that profit goals trump public health."

He sighed and said, "Sue, watch your back. Once the real culprits are caught, this mess will sort itself out. Your actions to save Reinhardt were heroic. But you need to stay the course. Their efforts to accuse your charitable company, Spot of Hope, of a personal motive for profit is pure bull. They'll never prove it because it just isn't so. I've seen the results of doctors and cancer patients that you've helped."

As she watched his gaze shift to an open journal, she realized she had taken too much time. Leaning forward, she said, "So you're telling me to stay sober, stay out of trouble, and keep my mouth shut."

With a broad smile, he stood, extended his hand, and said, "Did I say all that?"

"No, sir. As always, you just got me to say it."

Chapter 16

How dare those cops question her? Particularly the fat one from the university. Didn't they understand her plight? As Cindy teetered across her living room, she was so nervous she needed support from a nearby chair. Tossing the papers they'd served onto the glass coffee table, she dove for the sofa. Sinking into its soft cushions, she focused on slowing her heart. Years ago, she would have bluffed her way through their probing questions. But since her surgery, her thinking was faulty. Even the shake in her hands was worse. She knew they were out to get her. She needed to think. Then she remembered the pills in her sweater. Shaking out two yellow capsules, she swallowed them without water. Although it worsened the metal taste in her mouth, they soon would calm her.

As her vision cleared, she thought, What's the big deal? A few traced phone calls. That didn't mean anything. They couldn't prove a thing. Furthermore, she was home last Saturday night, all night long. At least, that's what she told them. How could they expect her to have witnesses? If they studied her face, they'd know—who would spend a Saturday night with her? Other than her secret online friend, the one she didn't tell them about.

That damn university cop, Stuhl. He'd smirked as if he didn't believe her. Then she showed him the snake, and it must have frightened him, because he left in less than a minute. But now there was a problem. She needed a new lawyer to handle their court appearance for harassment.

She strode to the small rolltop desk in the corner of the room, the area she called her study. She opened her laptop, knowing, as always, her friend would tell her what to do. Gingerly lowering herself onto the antique chair, she placed her pill bottle on the desk. As the pills worked their magic, she felt more in control. Her friend had suggested them, as well as others, which helped her through these harrowing times. He was better than any doctor. He fathomed her dilemma. She could never go out in public, so he had her medicines delivered to her. Now he needed to deliver a lawyer.

Jerking the cursor across a sea of icons, she located the one for their secret chat room. He said it was secret because it was part of the dark web. Of course, such technical terms were beyond her, but that's what she admired about him. He was so smart and loved her. They were mentally connected. He knew her needs. Clicking on the search box, she typed his name, Larpa369. Two minutes later, a pop-up screen appeared, saying, "Hi babe." They were now connected. She could count on him. When her had surgery failed, he was there, every night. It was his idea, how they would get revenge on Dr. Dreskin.

She typed, "Hi babe how r u? I miss u."

"Me 2."

"I heard it went grate the other nite. U really got em – good girl!!!"

"NP I told u I'd give em hell."

She smiled. Her friend was so wise. He helped her do things she couldn't possibly do alone. Like how to get those special nasty bees. He'd delivered them in a special box, along with the vial of queen bee aroma.

How great to have a secret friend. Someone to trust and confide in. Staring at the screen, she awaited his response and thought how easy it was to chat. No spelling, no grammar, no punctuation, all abbreviations. It was true: cyberspeak was the language of the future. It also had another advantage: no one could see your lies. Like telling him she was nineteen. But when she lied, she made it up by fulfilling his every online sexual fantasy.

When her screen beeped again, she saw that he had typed, "I really want u babe. Need you bad. R u dressed like I want??"

"Yes. Just like u told me."

"Good. Tell me what ur wearing. Tell me what you did as a beauty queen."

Chapter 17

Grace had left him for a week. They needed her back at the office in LA. This was his first time alone since the fire. Today, whenever his nurse entered his room, he had her check the airline flight schedule. Finally, she told him Grace's plane had landed in New York. As if he could hasten her arrival, he stared at the doorway and listened.

Suddenly, she burst into his life and said, "Guess who sees and hears every move our little Whitney makes?"

Despite his anticipation, he was caught off guard. "Who?"

"Well, Malcolm, I told you my guys were good."

"What happened?"

"Can you guess who spent the night in Whitney's apartment?"

"Probably the same guy who's still trying to get into her pants," he snarled. "Falcone."

"Better, Malcolm, much better." Not waiting for his response, she said, "One of my investigators. It took a little time, but he's in her apartment right now."

He felt the scars on his forehead tighten as he frowned. "I don't follow. He's in her apartment now?"

Laughing, she said, "Well, virtually, yes."

"What the hell do you mean?"

He heard her slap her knee. "Let's just say my boy Felix is good," she said. "A master hacker. Seems that Whitney needs her Starbucks coffee every morning. She also likes to read her email at the same corner table. Anyway, as she goes online, he taps into her network and sends her a message that she clicks on, believing she's deleting it. Unfortunately, it transferred control of her computer over to him. And he promptly filled it with spyware."

"Sounds like he screwed her better than Falcone. What will the Trojan virus give us?"

Hearing her heels click on the floor, he knew she was pacing when she said, "Not *will* give, but *has* given." In her best trial voice, she said, "It'll transmit all her email and anything stored on her hard drive. Plus her computer's camera and microphone will always be on. So we'll know who she talks to and maybe catch a compromising photo or two."

Rubbing the side of his face, he said, "And I take it that you learned something already."

"Oh, indeed we have. It appears Whitney communicates frequently with Falcone by email. She also spews horseshit about not seeing him romantically, not just yet, anyway." Then her pacing stopped, as if she'd struck an invisible wall. "It also seems Miss Whitney likes to keep up with the latest fashions at Victoria's Secret."

In spite of his hatred for Whitney, images of her slender frame, her almond-shaped eyes, and the way several strands of hair floated over one eye raced across his mind as he recalled questioning her on the witness stand. He wondered what sort of erotic thoughts she had, especially now in all this turmoil. If he hadn't been disfigured by fire, could he have used her fear as an excuse for a dinner meeting? Would she have accepted his invite? And then what next? Recalling stories from his colleagues in matrimonial law, he knew these relationships occurred all the time. So frequently, in fact, that the American Bar Association had passed an ethics ruling to discourage such behavior. At least while they were actively defending their client. But as a dull pain throbbed behind his unseeing eye, he knew, for him, such pleasures were a mirage.

"So what does her sex life have to do with our case?" he blurted.

Resuming her pacing, she said softly, "We're not sure yet. It's just dirt we might use at the right time. Destroy her Miss Perfect image, the one she loves to project."

"What about the emails to Falcone?"

"They're more interesting. Especially the one about meeting with Dr. Harrison, the chief of surgery. Evidently, they talked about Dr. Taylor, whom she hates, and why Dreskin lied for her when you were attacked. That's the main worry for both of them. It also explains my unexpected meeting in LA."

"Wait a minute. What meeting in LA?"

He judged she had stopped pacing and had taken a seat in her comfortable chair next to him as she said, "The chairman of the hospital board, Richard Cambridge, made a special trip to LA to meet with me. He wanted privacy. The board members, all business folks, are really concerned that the blowback from your incident, as they now call it, has stymied their application for a designated comprehensive cancer center."

"Like how?"

"There are two main groups who are gaining strength and threatening to deep-six their application. The first are the hospitals that already hold official designations. They've already submitted challenges about diluting the physician talent pool, compromising good public health, blah, blah, blah. But we know their real motive is keeping the money for themselves."

After a pause, she said, "The second group, and according to the chairman, the real pain, is their own hospital staff, probably inflamed by outsiders."

"What the hell are you saying? The staff is supporting the attack on me."

"Malcolm, slow down. Everyone wants justice, but it seems a little too slow for them. The board's interests are clear: get an approved application and then get the money. The staff of doctors and nurses are mostly liberal university do-gooders worried about ethics, morality, good public health, and then climate control, in that order."

"So what is the staff doing?"

"It appears that, like cats, they can't be herded. That plastic surgeon scumbag, Dreskin, is making noises and firing up students about how he's being unfairly targeted. The university student paper has written an editorial about fair hearings and rights. You've heard it all before. If they can do this to me, what will they next do to you?"

"And the board and business community don't see this as helping their application," he said.

"Correct. Plus the nurses and staff doctors fear, in the end, they will be blamed for your poor patient care. When shit rolls, it's always downhill. So one or more of them will get the ax."

"I see where this is going."

He heard her stand up, and several seconds later, there was the sound of clinking glassware. He wasn't sure, but he thought he heard a splash. He knew he was right when she said, "I know it's early, but I need a drink. Care for a bourbon?"

Still confused, he answered, "No."

Resuming her seat, she said, "We've got to end this thing fast. Whitney, I'm sure, is responsible for everything. That little bitch is smarter than we thought. There are just too many balls in the air. Deskin, either alone or with Whitney, attacked you in the hospital. And now these university professors are pontificating opinions that can cloud our goal."

Standing again, she sounded as if she was stamping her foot. "Malcolm, we've got to control this clusterfuck. We're too deep into it. And we have too much at stake."

Boldly, he said, "I got it. We need to connect or fabricate the lines connecting the dots. It's time we meet with that egotistical Dr. Taylor. He's president of the medical staff. We'll squeeze him to get the staff under control. Next, we need to link Whitney to that freak patient and then to Dreskin. We also need to splatter that bullshit company of hers, Spot of Hope. It should be easy for your Felix guy to screw up her financial records."

Finally, he felt warm and pushed his blanket aside. "Grace, it's time we get serious about revenge."

Chapter 18

Whenever she entered a chat room after midnight, the activity inside was electric. Ever since her surgery, whenever she couldn't sleep, she walked around the house until fatigue overwhelmed her. But soon that habit no longer worked; instead, the feeling that her skin was crawling overwhelmed her. That's when she turned to the internet.

At first, it was online shopping that held her attention. But soon everything looked alike. Exploring casino gambling was fun, but she quickly maxed out her credit card. Besides, those places required concentration, especially when playing Texas Hold'em poker. The only place to relax was a chat room. With so many available, it was difficult to choose one.

It was Dreskin, the butcher, who'd recommended medical websites. Before her surgery, she found them helpful, especially the links to patients who'd undergone similar procedures. But thanks to her skillful web navigation, she had discovered her special friend. Sometimes, when she didn't want to disturb him, she chose general interest chat rooms. But most of those topics bored her. Romance chat rooms were more exciting but filled with perverts.

Suddenly, her screen flashed a small window. It was their special secret room.

Jerking her cursor to it, she clicked it and typed, "Hi babe – horny?????"

"Always. Did u find a lawyer???"

She marveled at his love for her. He recognized her every need. He always came through. He never let her down. She had called over half the lawyers in the city and still couldn't find one. As soon as she described what Dreskin had done to her and then explained about the snake, they all said no. And then hung up. Those bastards Reinhardt and Peller—they had blackballed her.

She answered him, "No. Did u find one for me???"

"Hon u no I did!!!"

"Luv u – who??"

"Andrew Falcone…write down his address. 555 Main Street, Suite 801."

"Who's he??"

Before he answered, she clutched a pencil and pad and flipped pages to find a clean sheet. She smiled at the screen names she'd collected from last night's tour of a chat room for loving housewives. One name was circled: horhound402. Next to it she had scribbled, "He wants a pic."

Taking a moment to minimize the chat window, she clicked her photo folder, which layered a dozen thumbnails of her naked self-portraits. Pointing to the one of her stretched across the sofa, she double-clicked it to fill the screen. Admiring her leg draped over the armrest, she had to admit she had assets. Firm thighs, tapered calves, and a flat abdomen, thanks to a thousand sit-ups. Hugging the pillow behind her head projected her breasts like pillars. A stimulant for any man's desire.

But as she circled the cursor around her face, her anger boiled. As the cursor jittered, she clicked the magnifying icon to enlarge her face. Staring at the spray of hair near her ear, she clicked on enlarge and swore she saw the snake squirm. If only that butcher hadn't maimed her, it wouldn't have been necessary to use the Paint app and cover her face with a black splotch. She clicked the red X, and the image disappeared, exposing his frozen message awaiting her response.

She jotted Falcone's name and address and typed, "OK."

He answered, "He's the lawyer for the doc who lost her license – the one who beat up the bad congress guy."

With vague memories jumbled in her head, she typed, "What do I do??"

"Go to his office. Don't talk about Dreskin – just get him to defend u for bee stuff…"

"But I want him to get the butcher!!!"

"I no babe. Be patient – he's not that kinda lawyer. Just does defense."

Staring at his blurred words, she wondered, Why's he making me do this?

As if he'd read her mind, he typed, "Trust me babe – I take care of u – don't I???"

"Yes u do."

"Good. Now go see em. OK??? Just talk about the cops blamin u about Peller and bees."

"OK I will."

"Now what u wearin?"

Chapter 19

As Susan sat in Andy's waiting room, she gazed at the large table displaying assorted newspapers and magazines. The firm's annual report caught her attention. Lifting it and flipping through its pages, she paused at Andy's photograph. Below his picture was the title Founder and Senior Partner. As she inspected his photo more closely, she saw tinges of gray at his temples, more noticeable in the picture than in real life.

She recalled when they were fresh graduates from med and law school, both filled with energy, enthusiasm, and a certainty that their work would make a difference. But today he was a senior partner, and yesterday she'd received a letter from the state's health commissioner stating that her license would be revoked following review of her pending Article 78 proceedings before the public health council.

Andy's assistant entered the waiting room and said, "Dr. Whitney, please follow me."

As they walked down the corridor, she noticed surroundings she hadn't seen on her first visit. Entering his office, she scrutinized his expansive mahogany desk that reflected the sun like a mirror. The matching wooden cabinet, with beveled glass doors and filled with antique collectibles, also reflected his good taste. When he stood, she saw that his smile was the only thing that had remained, over the years, unchanged.

"Sue, I'm glad you agreed to meet here. It's better to handle your case here, not by phone or email. I'm concerned about several matters."

As she sank into a cushioned chair, she said, "Now that I've focused on your office decor, I'm certain I can't afford you." Attempting to recover, she added, "Whatever happened to your first office, the one behind the snack room?"

Swiveling his burgundy leather chair, he laughed. "We made a bigger snack room. By the way, can I get you something?"

"No, your opulence fills me, thanks."

Lost in self-pity, she recalled her father's admonition on using vile words, comparing them to a kite. A kite had a string, but once odious words were aloft, not even God could pull them back.

Gazing into his eyes, she said, "Andy, I'm sorry. I didn't mean it the way it sounded. I'm happy for you. You deserve success and more." She dropped her head. "I'm so defeated. I know it's hopeless, and I'm not sure I can fight it any longer."

He said, "Remember your college dorm room—sharing Chinese food as you tutored, or at least tried to tutor, me in chemistry?" He noted her smile. "Let's talk that way now. OK?"

She nodded, "Thanks, Andy. OK."

With a wrinkled forehead, he said, "Sue, there's something new and strange with your case."

"You mean like my letter from the health commissioner?"

"Not that. Something vague that I can't get my arms around." He reached into his desk drawer and yanked out a folder. "There's something about Reinhardt that doesn't make sense."

"Like what? I'm lost, Andy. What are you saying?"

"Yesterday, a woman came in without an appointment. Her head was wrapped in a huge black scarf. She demanded to see me urgently. She said she was referred by a close friend of mine. So I went out to see her."

As the creases on his forehead deepened, she tried to lighten the mood. "Well, you know that waiting room is so comfortable."

Grinning, he continued, "Anyway, she insisted I defend her on a harassment complaint initiated by Michael Peller." He gazed up from the folder. "Peller is Reinhardt's partner who was in the paper..."

"Yeah, I read it. Bee attack or something."

"Correct. But as I later learned, this woman was charged with making obscene phone calls to Peller's home."

"I still don't see where this is going."

"I'm also confused. But when I told her I don't handle such cases, she started pacing in circles around the room. My assistant was so frightened she called the police."

"And here I thought only the emergency room was odd on nights with a full moon."

Propping his elbows on the desk, he said, "You'd be surprised what we see here. Anyway, when my assistant came back and announced the cops were coming, the woman freaked and screamed that I was protecting that butcher Dreskin. Then she bolted outside."

"Did the cops find her?"

"Don't know. But later that day, your favorite inspector, Stuhl, stopped by."

After a deep breath, she said, "That's strange. What did Stuhl want?"

Glaring at her, he said, "Not much, really. He asked about the incident and if the woman confessed to the Peller attack. I'm sure the cops think she did it."

"So have the cops charged her?"

"Not to my knowledge, which is also a little strange. Stuhl beat around the bush and implied he wasn't convinced about the evidence."

She shook her head. "How is this connected to my case?"

Lifting a new thick folder, he said, "I've outlined the pros and cons of your case. Let's go over them."

She slid forward in her chair. "Great. Shoot."

"OK, on the pro side, I've filed an Article 78 with the state, which explains your letter from the health commissioner. You can't practice medicine in the hospital, but your license is still probationary. At least that gives you some presumption of innocence."

"Not much, but something," she said.

"The con side is bigger. There are two major hurdles. First are the pending charges dealing with the university claims of fraud, theft of services, and using their equipment for your private company. That's mostly bullshit. However, their claims of diversion of federal grant funds will require substantial defense on your part."

"None of that stuff is true," she said adamantly. "I never received any federal grant funds."

He nodded. "We know that's true, but in legal matters, we need proof, which takes time to gather. The second major hurdle is more serious. It targets you for the criminal assault on Reinhardt, conspiracy with others for the house explosion, and the Peller attack. Indictment and conviction on any of these charges carries a lengthy jail term."

She frowned. "Got it. So what do we do?"

Extracting some new papers, he said, "Let's drill deeper into my suspicions and our defense plan. The house explosion and the assumption that Jane Reinhardt's death was a suicide to pay back Malcolm for his philandering is unproven. She had stage five cancer with little time left. So it's possible she might have committed suicide. The Feds would need to prove otherwise to convict you."

"How would they do that?"

"I've verified that the ATF oversees that part of the investigation, and they sent a load of material to their Fire Research Laboratory in Atlanta, Georgia. That move could be good or bad for us. It takes us away from the local cops, whom I don't trust."

"Well. I certainly didn't blow their house up."

"We know that. But they could contend you had a partner. Also, I'm concerned about leaks I've heard from my colleagues. They tell me the hospital and university are planning some new cancer center. There's a lot of local inside trading behind this effort. I'm suspicious if the university fraud charges intend to associate you with certain investors who may have conflicts of interest."

"I know nothing about plans for a major cancer center. But I'm low on the food chain."

He shook his handful of papers as if new information would fall out. "Plus this second assault on Reinhardt in the hospital. Why? If the attacker managed all the hurdles to sneak into his room, why not just inject the battery acid into an IV line and kill him? Why all this torture stuff?" Andy looked a little nauseated. "I mean, that took real hatred."

Gazing upward as if just hearing his own words for the first time, he continued, "Which is exactly the foundation of the prosecutor's case against you. They are trying to prove your motive was blind animus."

"Believe me, Andy, I know that."

"And finally, there's all this crap about bee attacks and this crazy woman suing Dreskin. It's just suspicious to me that Stuhl is so focused on that part of the case. I've spoken to the federal prosecutor—not the assistant prosecutor but the boss. He doesn't have all the facts, but he says Stuhl has a strong gut feeling. And so they've given him free rein to lead the investigation."

"His gut is big enough," she grumbled. "Perhaps a laxative might clear his head."

Deaf to her barbs, he organized the folders on his desk. "So that's my analysis thus far."

He gazed at her, "Uh-oh, I know that look, Sue. What are you thinking up?"

Sliding to the edge of her seat, she said, "I recall your advice to shut up. To not discuss anything that we talk about with anyone else so that we preserve such information under attorney–client privilege. But I think I can get this crazy woman to talk to me."

Before Andy's eyebrows reached his scalp, she said, "Now hear me out. Everyone seems to agree this woman is crazy. Yet there are moments when she carries out rather complex tasks, like the bee attack. Plus she is hyperfocused on one person: Dreskin. It would be a waste of time to pump him for information. But she's weak minded enough that I might learn something. In addition, I can gain her sympathy by playing the card that both of us have suffered similar persecution."

Andy stood and started to pace behind his chair, a sure sign of him thinking. Then he turned. "Sue, I can't let you do this. It's too dangerous. It could backfire and really raise their suspicions on you."

"That's your legal advice. But is it tainted by your feelings for me?"

"OK, then please don't do it, because I'm asking you not to."

She walked over to him, took his hand, and kissed his cheek as softly as a butterfly might land with sore feet. "You've been my rock and helped me so many times. Please support me here. I promise I'll be careful."

And then, as swiftly as she'd kissed him, she left the office.

Before she reached the elevator, she saw him race toward her with something in his hand. "Sue," he said. "You forgot your laptop."

Chapter 20

After the fire, Malcolm had no visitors other than his sister and Inspector Stuhl. But this morning was special. He was about to receive his first invited guest. Also another first in a long time: he put on his favorite gray Armani suit with an off-white shirt left open at the neck for a casual business look. Seated in his recliner, he tucked his hands beneath the wool blanket covering him from his knees down to his black oxford shoes. Awaiting his guest, he turned his head toward the window to let the sun warm scattered patches of skin.

Grace focused his thoughts when she said, "Remember, let me direct the conversation. We want him to believe this is a career opportunity."

He cleared his throat. "Yeah, and from what you've told me, his ego, coupled with his greed for fame and money, should make him putty in our hands."

"He's a true deontologist. Pompous enough to believe only he can set the rules for right and wrong." She gave a sardonic laugh. "Not unlike many academic doctors we know."

The feeble knock on the door stopped their conversation. Malcolm heard Grace's heels stab the floor as she strode over to admit their guest. Then he heard her say, "Dr. Taylor, please come in."

Malcolm allowed time for the shuffle of their feet to cease, and he imagined Taylor's anxiety. Holding his silence, he wondered if Taylor was gazing at anything in the room in order to avoid looking at Malcolm's face.

Grace broke the moment, saying, "Of course you remember my brother, don't you?"

Taylor struggled with a cough and said, "Yes. How are you, Mr. Reinhardt?"

"Not well, Doctor. But we hope you can help us."

"That's why we invited you here, Doctor," Grace said, adopting her formal attorney voice. "And I trust we can speak freely."

"Please know, I—I want to help in any way that I can," he stammered. "But please understand the hospital's attorney advised against my coming."

"Forget him," snapped Grace.

Malcolm said, "Doctor, are you aware of our litigation against the hospital for gross negligence? Soon we will be filing additional litigation against several doctors. But I want you to understand that our prime concern is justice."

"Dr. Taylor, let me speak bluntly," Grace said. "What is your assessment of Dr. Whitney?"

The pause was so long, Malcolm thought he could hear Taylor sweating. At last he said, "She's a cavalier, smart-mouthed surgeon."

Plucking his hand from beneath the blanket, Malcolm made a fist, as best as his deformed fingers would allow, and then said, "Doctor, don't bullshit me. We're not interested in her medical skills. Nor are we here to give her an award. We need to know—did she do this?" With his one good finger, he pointed to his face.

"We know you're her critic," Grace said in a raised voice. "Plus you oversaw her that night." She paused for several seconds. "Legally speaking, one could argue you are responsible for her actions and their consequences."

Malcolm knew from his courtroom experience that pressure on a witness had to be applied skillfully. They must be humiliated, devastated, and nearly destroyed, but at the last critical moment, they must be given a path to redemption. Be turned into an ally.

Taking the baton from his sister, he gently said, "Dr. Taylor, I know you want to help. And I know of your loyalty to the hospital and university. But we believe, as we suspect you do, Whitney caused my deformity. Her actions could topple your fine hospital, as well as limit your career—say, for example, your promotion to executive vice president for health affairs."

Certain that Taylor's eyes must be wide as saucers, Malcolm continued, "So tell me, Doctor, has she ever spoken ill of me? Perhaps blaming me for all her problems?"

Speaking like a best friend forever, Grace added, "You understand that anything you tell us—we'll treat it as confidential."

Taylor blurted, "After rehab, she was screwed up." He took an audible dry swallow. "It was like she couldn't shake her past. I mean, it was as if she couldn't get it out of her head."

"Like what?" asked Malcolm.

"I never wanted her back in the hospital. I told them so. But Harrison came to her defense. He argued for another chance, and the hospital caved in."

Again Malcolm bellowed, "We don't care about her social history. Did she ever make threats about me? Was she doing something on the side? Give it up, man; don't waste our time."

Grace said in a matching voice, "And we don't like to have our time wasted."

"There were rumors," Taylor said. "About what she owed guys."

"What do you mean?" shrieked Malcolm.

"When she drank a lot, she had men, lots of men. There were stories of a little cocaine. When she left rehab, some of those men, some nurses, wanted to continue. You know, get her to steal a little drug from the pharmacy. We heard there were threats to expose her if she didn't."

"That little bitch," Grace said. "I knew she was a slut."

"Anyway," said Taylor, "there was never any proof. The hospital investigated thoroughly. But one night while she was working, I caught her crying. She was talking to one of the female nurses about you."

He heard Grace slap the table as she said, "What did she say?"

"That it was your fault. You brought this on her. That Congressman Rye was unethical, but you were the real scum for defending him."

Grace muttered, "That bitch."

Calmly, as when a witness had delivered everything he wanted, Malcolm said, "Thank you, Doctor. Now that wasn't so hard, was it?"

Waving his hand, with two bent fingers pointing to the door, he signaled that the meeting was over. Listening to the shuffle of feet, he added, "Perhaps, Doctor, we'll chat again."

Hearing the lock snap shut, Malcolm said, "Yes, Dr. Taylor, we'll chat again. In court. You'll be a fine witness."

Grace sat next to him and laughed. And once again, he stretched his facial scars until they hurt, and he laughed with her.

When they both paused, he said, "I guess you were right. Our little Dr. Whitney is more criminal than we knew."

"Indeed. And now, thanks to the bug in her laptop, we know what they're planning."

Chapter 21

Using her thumb like a knife, Cindy stabbed the power button on her computer. She had been betrayed. Why had he sent her there? That lawyer Falcone was a loser. He didn't give one hoot about her. As icons flashed before her, the cursor juggled off the screen. Placing two hands on the mouse, she recaptured the cursor and centered it. Then, moving it with two hands, she placed it over their secret icon. A double click brought up the window for their private chat room as she hissed, "It's early, but you better be on."

Staring at the open window, she typed, "U there???"

Her message remained marooned on a blank dark screen.

Glancing at her watch, she cursed him. He should be on. As the cursor began shivering, she reached for another yellow capsule. She shook the bottle upside down, but nothing fell out. Staggering from her chair, she scurried to her bedroom upstairs. Opening the top drawer, she flipped its contents onto the bed. Tearing through underwear, bras, and assorted jetsam, she spotted a spare brown bottle. Struggling with the childproof cap, she ripped it off and shook out four yellow capsules. Loosely replacing the plastic cap, she placed the bottle atop the bureau. Dashing into the bathroom, she splashed water into a cup and swallowed the pills in one gulp. Rubbing her eyes with balled fists to build her courage, she then peered into the mirror and screamed, "Oh my God!"

Squeezing both eyes shut, she shook her head, convinced she was still asleep. Slowly, she cracked open one eye, then the other. Through a veil of eyelashes, she turned her head from side to side to view the snake. And then, just like her dear friend had predicted, the drug began to work. Fully opening both eyes, she saw the snake was gone. Or maybe he had just crawled under her hair. Carefully lifting a curl, she spotted his head. He was quiet and coiled. Ever so gently, she laid the curl back down. The snake didn't move. Dropping her hand, she backed away from the mirror and averted her gaze.

Clutching the handrail with two hands, she tramped down the stairs. Approaching her computer, she giggled at the screen, which displayed his name, Larpa369, and his greeting. "Hi babe…"

Dropping onto the chair, she pounded the keyboard as she typed, "He was useless…no help…an asshole."

"What happened???"

"He did nothing…called the cops. I ran out."

"Easy babe. U sound excited. How u feel????"

"Nervous, very shaky. The snake is moving…I'm afraid. Don't want cops back here. What should I do?????"

"Which capsules did u take??"

"The yellow ones…They worked before."

"U need something stronger…I'll get u some today. Be patient."

Leaning back in her chair, she sighed, as her jumbled thoughts stopped banging together. But gazing at the monitor, she saw it grow dimmer. Bringing her face closer until her nose nearly touched the screen, she typed, "What do I do now???"

"What are u wearing babe???"

"No no…not yet…What we do bout him…the lawyer???"

"He was bad, very bad to do that…we need to teach him a lesson…OK??"

Her heart raced. "Yes but what??"

"Need to plan something…u no I never let u down…we'll get Falcone and his girlfriend doctor too…Trust me babe???"

"Yes, OK."

"Good girl. Now what u wearing??"

Suddenly, the sound of the doorbell shattered the mood. She stopped typing. She wasn't certain of the sound or where it had come from until it rang again, much longer this time. Gazing at the keyboard and perhaps seeking a pathway out, she typed, "Gotta go – doorbell."

She saw a reply flash across her screen, but she ignored it.

Approaching the front window, she dropped to her knees and gently slid the heavy drape aside. Peeking through the narrow opening, she spotted the figure's back. It was a woman. Cindy watched the woman lean on the bell again. But this time she also pounded on the door. When the knocking stopped, she heard, "Ms. Franklin, I know you can hear me. My name is Dr. Susan Whitney. I need to speak with you. Those people after you are also after me. I think we can help each other."

Ever so cautiously, she stood and crept toward the door. Peering through the peephole, she had no sense of fear. Unlatching the bolt, she opened the door. For several seconds, they each stared at one another. Susan spoke first. "Cindy, I'm so glad to meet you. We both have suffered so much. I believe I can help you, as you can me."

Standing like a stone in the doorway, Cindy scrutinized her visitor from head to toe. Susan then said, "May I come in so we can chat?"

Chapter 22

As Cindy backed away from the doorway. Susan slid by her to get inside. She sauntered toward the green couch in the room's center and said, "Let's sit for a moment."

Susan gently guided Cindy's arm as they both strolled to the couch. When they were seated, Cindy asked, "How can you help me? And why do you want to? Did that butcher Dreskin hurt you?"

Before answering, Susan noticed messages flashing across the computer's screen, which was too far away to read at the end of the room. Then she said, "Yes, Dr. Dreskin has hurt me, but in a very different way than what happened to you. I'm here to see what I can do for you." With a grin, she added, "As they say, we girls need to stick together."

As Cindy squeezed her shaking hands still, Susan saw her eyes dance from side to side beneath her drooping lids. Perhaps trying to clear her vision, Cindy began to blink like a flashing stoplight. As if she was dizzy, she tightly closed her lids. Then Susan said, "Sit still. I'll get you a glass of water."

Susan strode to the far doorway, which she hoped would lead to the kitchen. It did. And it also permitted her to pass the computer. Pausing for a moment, she read: "No no stop…don't answer…stop!!" Each line had the screen name Larpa369.

Entering the kitchen, she pulled out a pen from her jacket and wrote the name in her pocket notepad. In the kitchen sink, she saw dirty plates, utensils, frying pans, and glasses, one of which was broken, all piled upon one another. Opening several cupboards to find a glass, she encountered various pill bottles. Behind four coffee cups, there was a small brown bottle. Darting back to the doorway, she peeked at Cindy. She was still seated and rubbing her head like a dog might scratch its ear. Opening the brown bottle, Susan poured out two yellow capsules and placed them in her pocket. The next cabinet revealed a glass. After clearing away two plates caked with egg and a pan burned with crusted meat, Susan filled the glass with water from the faucet.

Returning to the couch, she offered Cindy the water and said, "Please drink this. It will help."

Cindy answered, "I think I need my medicine."

"Not right now, Cindy. What kind of medicine do you take?" No sooner had she said it than she realized it was a mistake.

Cindy stood and began to pace. "It's special medicine. Not something that crooked doctors would give out. I got it from my friend. They're working too. To help me get rid of the snake." Placing her glass of water on the table with a thud, she blurted, "This water tastes like metal. What did you put in it? Who sent you here? You're not here to help me. You're one of those doctors, aren't you?"

As her pacing became more erratic, she began to swish her arms wildly, as though the room were filled with bees. With Andy's words burning in her ears, Susan moved toward the front door and pleaded, "Cindy, you need help now. Let me call the hospital."

"Get out, you fucking bitch! You're like the rest of them. Get out before I kill you!"

Fortunately, the front door was still ajar, so Susan raced through it. Striding down the front porch steps, she heard the door slam shut, followed by a litany of muffled curses.

Chapter 23

As soon as Cindy slammed the door and locked it, she was exhausted. Even in her foggy state, she knew she had made a mistake. Why had she trusted that wretched doctor? Because she was female? Shaking her head, she thought, How stupid. She was too kind, too trusting. Even Congressman Rye had told her that. He said, "In Washington politics, people never care about what you did for them yesterday. It's only what you can do for them today."

He had given her many life lessons, like, "Never trust a person from the opposite political party. If you think that by helping them you'll become their friend, forget it. They will cut your heart in a single beat. There is no loyalty; it's always about payback. Hurt me today, and no matter how long it takes, I'll get my revenge."

Perhaps the most difficult lesson she'd had to absorb was his view on how to deal with everyone, friend or foe. He said, "Most importantly, remember this: if there is no downside to hurting you, people will continue to screw you."

Once Congressman Rye had read her a passage from the biography of William Bligh, captain of the HMS *Bounty* in 1789. Bligh's favorite quote was, "Now don't mistake me. I'm not advising brutality with no purpose. My point is that cruelty with purpose is not cruelty—it's efficiency. Then a man will never disobey, once he's watched his mate's backbone laid bare. He'll see the flesh jump, hear the whistle of the whip for the rest of his life."

As she paced erratically around her living room, clutching a chair for balance, she pondered how she could recall all these quotes. Shaking a fist into the air, she said aloud, "I'm a Vassar graduate. I was and still am somebody.

Why is this happening to me? I should have stayed in Washington. I was more than an airhead beauty pageant runner-up."

Ambling back to her computer, she hoped that her friend was still online. He could help her sort this out. Staring at the screen, she scrolled through his stream of unread texts, which ended with, "Stop – Don't answer!!!!"

Quickly, she typed, "I'm back babe. U there?"

She wrung her hands for a couple minutes that seemed like an hour. At last her screen lit up with, "KK. Wait – brb."

Feeling her heart slow and the tremor in her hands subside, she knew he would be right back. Wiggling the cursor around icons on the screen, she slowly felt her anger boil. That butcher Dreskin had really hurt her. If it weren't for him, she would have a normal relationship with Larpa369. No more of these online hookups. She could fully give herself to him. He was so kind. He was always there, and he helped. Not like the others. Yet she was doomed to only serve him virtually.

At last he replied. But his new message didn't make sense. Rubbing her eyes several times, she thought it must be the medicine. Or worse yet, it probably was the snake. She read the message again. "U dumbass bitch. I hate u!!!"

She gaped at the screen as more lines followed. "U r useless. A piece of shit. How stupid can u be??? I helped u. But now no more. Let the snakes get u...and they will. There are two snakes, one on each side. The other is growing, and they both will go in your ears."

Frantically, she typed, "No babe. I luv u...Why r u doing this? Help me..."

"Go to hell. The snakes will start eating ur cerebral cortex. U will go mad. Then they will move to ur cerebellum. U will no longer walk. Then, as a cripple, u will lie alone on the floor as the snakes chew ur brain stem. Ur heart will beat faster and faster. Then the snakes will feast on ur medulla to destroy ur breathing. And finally, u will die, and I will be rid of u, the most useless, ugly bitch I ever saw."

She felt as if her body had turned to stone, her mind crumbled into fragments. His next text was a blur. "BTW bitch, don't ever contact me again. And for ur dumb brain, we chat on a nontraceable dark web site. Plus I just activated a computer virus that will mix up ur hard drive worse that ur stupid brain."

Suddenly, her screen flashed brighter than ever before. And she wondered, Is this what's called the blue screen of death?

Chapter 24

Susan fled from Cindy's house. She jumped into her car and headed to the medical lab for an analysis of the capsules. Pulling into a parking spot reserved for doctors, she made her way inside, hoping that her friend Rita, the lab's director, would be there. She was. After expressing to the receptionist the urgency of seeing the director, she was escorted to her office.

Once inside, and slightly out of breath, she said, "Rita, I need your confidence, trust, and your help, desperately."

"Whoa, girlfriend, sit down. And yes, you got it. Now what the hell is going on?"

Susan gave a long sigh. "I can't tell you all the details because I'm in deep shit. But if you read the daily press, you know just how deep it is. However, what I'm going to ask—it's critical to my case. And if I'm being truthful, it could mean trouble for you."

"OK, girl, shoot."

Extracting one of the capsules, she said, "I need an analysis of this ASAP. I'm certain there's a heavy-metal contaminant. Again, the test results need to be kept top secret."

Rita put the capsule in a lab bottle. "OK, I got it. Don't worry about secrecy." With a smile, she added, "Now get yourself a coffee—best it be decaf—and take a seat in our sparse waiting room."

Trying to calm down, Susan pondered her future, which she had just made worse. Perhaps she should return to Iowa and become a family doctor. Certainly she would never get hospital privileges anywhere. Plus a license suspension from New York would prejudice a license in any state. Perhaps becoming an Uber driver was a better choice.

Her favorite aunt, Jessie, had said all along, "Sue, forget all those years of schooling. Surgery isn't a job for women. If you want to put that Columbia University degree in liberal arts to use, finish med school and become a dermatologist. But if you're going to do that, it's a lot faster to become a hairdresser. I mean, some of them give Botox and all sorts of skin treatments. Shucks, I've seen TV ads where they offer mini face-lifts for baggy eyes and turkey necks. My God, they're the same as plastic surgeons but in less time. And I'll bet their malpractice insurance is cheaper. And you know, hon, the real advantage is you can do that job part-time, which means you can focus on raising a family. Now that's a job with benefits for life."

The sudden ring of her cell phone vaporized her memories. She answered softly.

"Hi, Sue, Ray Dreskin here."

Catching her breath, she wondered what he could possibly want.

He said, "I thought you might be feeling a little down. So I thought of giving you a call. Could I drop over to see you?"

Despite her silence, he continued, "I have an idea that might be helpful."

"Like what?" she finally asked.

"I'd rather not discuss it over the phone. And since we've been warned not to meet, could I come over to your place, say about six o'clock?"

Sighing, she said, "I guess, I have a lot of free time now. OK, I'll text you my address."

As she speculated what was on his mind, Rita opened the waiting room door and waved her to follow. Entering her private office, Susan waited as Rita closed the door.

"Where the hell did you get this?" Rita asked.

After a long pause, Susan said, "Girlfriend, I just can't tell you that right now. But trust me, it's vital for my case."

"OK. You owe you. But this shit could get me fired. I'll keep it off the books. Thank goodness I filled out a bullshit number for the computer. Anyway, it's what you suspected. It's mercury in a very high dose. The capsule container was obtained from some health food store. But the contents are not vitamins. They're over 50 percent mercury with about 30 percent barbiturates, and the remainder is standard Valium."

"Holy shit, that's unreal."

"I sure as hell hope no one was taking these. 'Cause they will be screwed up, permanently."

Susan hugged her friend. "Thanks, babe, I owe you big time. But I've got to run."

Susan strode back to her car and closed the door, which momentarily snagged her coat, and pressed the icon for Andy's cell.

He answered with, "Hey, what's up?"

"I need to see you stat—."

"Yeah, I know. I've been waiting for you, just like we talked about. I have that Chinese food you like. And I'm starving, so get over here now."

Before she could even wonder what he was talking about, he ended the call.

Had mercury rubbed off in her brain? She started the car and headed to his office. When she arrived, his assistant was waiting at the door and immediately brought her to Andy's office. Before the assistant let Susan in, she said, "Mr. Falcone asked that you not say a word after I open his door."

As the door opened, Andy frantically waved at her to stand still. He brought his index finger to his tightly pursed lips, tapped them repeatedly, then directed her to sit down. As she did so, she noticed the strange copper box on his desk. Two wires ran from this box to an adjacent black box, which had flashing red LED lights. Convinced that everyone had ingested mercury, she felt herself turn to stone. Andy grabbed the strap of her shoulder bag and tugged it off. Fishing through it, he found her phone and again tapped his lips. He opened the door to the copper box and inserted the phone. Then, dropping to one knee, he seized her laptop and just as quickly placed it inside the copper box.

Clutching her arm, he towed her out the office door. A short distance down the corridor, they entered a small conference room. Feeling lighter but more comfortable, she said, "OK. Now what the hell?"

"Sue, I'm sorry for the intrigue, but a lot of serious things have happened."

"Not as serious as mine, I'll bet."

"I'll start anyway. That copper box in my office is an old-time but effective

Faraday cage. It blocks radio waves. My security guys are in my office now, hooking it to the black box for transport. I have a strong suspicion your phone and laptop have been bugged. I think our conversations have been tapped, and worse yet, I believe your computer speaker and camera are permanently on."

"Oh, great. So is my next job an online porn star?"

"Not funny, Sue. But this morning I was in the prosecutor's office, and they made a special effort to warn me about you. To make certain that you're not contacting any targets or witnesses. Later, when I pulled aside one of his assistants, she let it slip that they knew you met Cindy Franklin this morning."

After a distinct pause, he said, "Now how could anyone know that, other than me? Either they are following you twenty-four seven, which I doubt—they don't have the manpower—or you've been bugged. But if so, who did it? My security team will know the results shortly. With luck we might even learn what they copied off your hard drive."

"Holy crap, Andy, what do we do next?"

"Well, I have more to tell you, but you were so excited to tell me about your day. So please go ahead."

"Andy, have you ever heard of Mad Hatter's disease?"

"What I know is from, I think, *Alice in Wonderland* and the funny characters at the tea-party table."

"Well, they were funny in the movie, but not in real life."

Extracting the remaining capsule from her jacket, she placed it on the table and said, "I took this and one other capsule from a medicine bottle in Franklin's kitchen. Evidently, she has many of these hidden around the house. I had the one capsule analyzed. It's 50 percent mercury. Mercury is a serious brain poison. And Cindy has all the signs of advanced toxicity—metallic taste, tremors, unsteady gait, severe paranoia. She's a classic case."

"How did Franklin get these pills? And from where?"

"She rambled on about some online friend. She believes he loves her. He helps her by sending her these capsules to control the snake. A snake she imagines has risen from the raised scar in front of her ear. A snake she also insists crawls *into* her ear."

"Oh, this is nuts. What about this online pervert? Any info there?"

She pulled her notepad from her jacket. "I did get a glance at her computer screen. There were a series of words—'Stop, don't answer.' She must have been online when I arrived. I think whoever it was didn't want her to let me in. Anyway, this character's screen name is Larpa369."

As Andy scribbled down the name, he said, "My guys will need to check this out."

"Andy, my main concern is this woman is sick, very sick, and in need of immediate medical help. We need to get her to a hospital right now. Can you call someone?"

Shaking his head, he said, "Like who? The cops and prosecutor who just warned me about your witness tampering?"

"Forget them. We've got to help her."

"Sue, my first obligation is to you. The prosecutor also dropped that Inspector Stuhl's famous gut feeling is peaking. He reports serious irregularities in your company books for Spot of Hope."

"Screw him; he's an asshole. There's nothing there. For God's sake, it's a charity. We've more important things to worry about. Like helping this poor woman who's obviously being poisoned."

Starting to pace, as he always did when nervous, he said, "All right, give me a few minutes, and I'll try to figure out how we can get her help without implicating you."

"Oh, and by the way, regarding the prosecutor's concern over witness tampering. You might let him know that Ray Dreskin called me while I was waiting in the lab for the test results."

"What did he want?"

"Not sure, but he insisted he had some important idea to discuss that would help me. He's coming to my place at six o'clock."

"Dammit, Sue, you can't be doing this. They're getting set to indict you. You could wind up as the only target."

"All the more reason for me to help myself. I just can't stand being a pawn. But I promise I'll be careful. I'll just listen to what he has to say. And since I've been debugged, there will be no phone or laptop."

With an air of frustration, he said, "OK. Just listen to me. I'll try to get Ms. Franklin help. I don't know how yet, but I'll try." Then he reached into his pocket, took out his cell phone, and gave it to her. "I don't want you traveling alone and out of touch. My phone and office have been swept, so the phone is clean. I'll use my secure office cell phone while you have my personal one. If you need help, you can reach me."

"Thanks, Andy," she said with a smile. "But if I do receive a client call, can I bill by the hour just like you do?"

"Get out of here! And please stay out of trouble, at least for today."

Chapter 25

Still anxious over Cindy Franklin's health, Susan brewed some green tea as she awaited Ray Dreskin's arrival. With Andy's warnings churning in her mind, she pondered how Franklin's situation was, or could be, connected to her predicament. Was it a fluke occurrence or a Machiavellian plot? Dreskin had lied to the cops about being with her when Reinhardt's assault occurred. His reasons for doing this remained a puzzle.

While squeezing a bit of lemon into her tea, she heard a knock on her apartment door. Opening it, she found Ray Dreskin dressed in a dark blue, lightly pin-striped suit and vest and a red power tie. He smiled and proffered six long-stemmed red roses. Noticing her confused expression, he quickly said, "They're just a sign of friendship. I thought you could use a little cheer."

Taking the flowers, she said, "How nice. I appreciate the thought, Ray, but very little can cheer me up."

Nodding at the couch for him to sit, she trekked into the kitchen for a vase. "So what's this idea you have?"

"It's Malcolm Reinhardt's sister."

Stuffing the roses into a glass vase, she squeezed the bundle under the faucet and half filled it with water. As she placed it on the counter, a thorn pricked her finger, and she yelled, "Ouch…what are they up to now?"

Moving into the living room, she sat on the chair opposite him as he said, "My partner, Tom, overheard Reinhardt's sister talking about you to that Detective Stuhl."

"What did she say?"

"He didn't hear everything, but it seems the sister was trashing you. He heard things like, 'She was in the hospital during the attack'; 'her bogus company'; 'she's defrauding the university.'"

"I'm accustomed to the Reinhardts' diatribes. He's been after me for years." Although, she wondered, could these new attacks be connected to the tap on her phone and computer?

"Tom didn't have a clue either, but he was pretty certain she was pissed. He said the way she was pointing her finger in Stuhl's face—it was over the top. Anyway, I thought you should be aware and watch yourself."

"Well, thanks, Ray, I will." She stood and went to the kitchen. "Can I get you some coffee or tea?"

He followed her. "Sure, coffee and cream would be great." Then he said, "I don't know what those damn Reinhardts have against us. He's been on my butt for years. May God have mercy on me, but I wish the bastard had died."

Placing the kettle on the range, she slid a carton of cream toward him and said, "Reinhardt never forgave me after my TV appearances. I was critical of him, and I was angry. His client, Congressman Rye, was pushing legislation to deregulate oversight of health-insurance companies and to privatize more medical labs, of which he owned a chain. He was wrong, and Reinhardt was his attack dog."

"Yup, like all lawyers."

"Anyway, he's been after me for a long time."

As she hit the button on the automatic coffee maker, he said, "It appears the sister has taken up his malpractice banner."

"What do you know about her?"

"Other than that she's some hot-dog West Coast lawyer, not much."

He tested a sip of his coffee. "I'll see if Tom can learn more." Then he asked, "So what are your plans?"

Pouring fresh tea into a white ceramic cup adorned with red roses, she answered, "I'll need to find work. That's for sure. My favorite aunt fronted me a loan that'll carry me till next month, but after that…" She paused to regain her composure. "My legal bills are mounting every month. Coupled with my student loan payments, I just don't see a way out."

"Sue, I think I have a way out."

"I appreciate your thoughts, Ray. But I really can't accept..."

Reaching across the table, he squeezed her hand and said, "Trust me. There're no strings attached. Here's what I did. Does the name Annalee Jackson sound familiar to you?"

"No, not really."

He sat up straighter. "She's the vice-chairwoman of both the hospital and university board of directors. She also is a cosmetic patient of mine."

"OK. I'm impressed. Because I'm a trauma surgeon, 40 percent of my patients are uninsured felons with gunshot wounds."

"Seriously, Sue, my plan can help you. I met with Annalee the other day to tell her that I'm certain you're being framed for something you didn't do. I also touted your philanthropic website, SpotofHope.com, and your podcasts that help cancer patients undergoing surgery, radiation, and chemotherapy. I'm aware that the hospital and three universities are partnering to build a comprehensive cancer center. I explained how your work could add value to their application. You already have a few thousand online followers, and you have a gift for expressing empathy that encourages cancer patients to follow through with treatment."

Tightening her grip on her teacup, she gazed up at him and said, "Thanks, Ray, that was kind of you. But remember, I'm still damaged goods."

"Be that as it may, she called me back after meeting with her board chairman, Richard Cambridge, and expressed interest in my idea. They recognize they can't influence your criminal investigation, which could drag on for years if you're indicted. But they said they would meet with your attorney to buy your website, and its educational material and podcasts, for a sum of $3 million."

"Are you kidding me?"

"No. And of course they had some conditions. Your name could no longer be associated with Spot of Hope. However, for one year, you could be employed as a writer with a pseudonym for their podcasts and other materials. After one year your continued employment would be negotiable. If you're cleared by the FBI, they would bring you back using your real name."

As her eyebrows shot upward and her eyes widened like gunports on a ship, she raised her hand to stop him. "Why would they want to do this? I'm in the news every few days. There are tons of rumors about me, and they will only get worse. So I'm confused. I really can't think about that right now."

He took a gulp of his coffee. "When the cops find the real culprit, don't you think everyone, including the hospital, will owe you a big apology? Not to mention one hell of a compensation package?"

Meeting his gaze, and knowing she was innocent, she had to admit his point had merit. Besides, she deserved to be made whole again. After taxes, her legal bills would consume a hefty portion of any $3 million package. If she was indicted, who could predict the costs? But her guiding principle had always been no risk, no gain. So, as in the past, when life seemed darkest, an opportunity appeared. At first it might not seem promising, but then it blossomed.

As if he'd read her thoughts, he said, "This opportunity to work undisturbed, behind the scenes, without constant public scrutiny, would also keep your hands in medicine. So give it a chance."

She smiled. "I'll think seriously about it. OK?"

Glancing at his watch, he stood and said, "I need to get going. I'll call you in a couple days to hear your decision."

As she escorted him to the door, he paused and said, "Oh, speaking of calling you. Do you have a new phone number? I called earlier to let you know I might be a couple minutes late. But there was no answer nor any way to leave a voice message."

"Oh yeah, I lost my phone, so I'll be getting a new one with a new number. God knows who might find my old one and try to use it. I'll send out a private blast message to let friends know my new number."

As she closed the door behind him, she leaned against the frame and realized she had few options. The legal bills were mounting. The past month alone, her paralegal bills were over $20,000. Andy had only sent bills for office copying, document preparation, and assorted federal filing fees—another $6,000. Feeling adrift, she imagined the schadenfreude her enemies were savoring. Better than having to beg strangers for a job, Dreskin's offer was at least private, not to mention more profitable. Shaking her head, she wished there were another way. But there wasn't.

As she entered her bedroom, preparing to go to bed, she noticed Andy's phone on her nightstand. She lifted it, and the voicemail icon signaled five missed calls. Tapping it, she listened to Andy's troubled voice say, "Sue, I'm out of the office for several hours. Tried to reach you five times. Wanted you to know Cindy Franklin is dead. She hurled herself in front of an Amtrak train." After a brief pause, he added, "Sue, I want you to know I sent my security team to her house. She wasn't home, and no one could find her. I'm sorry. We'll talk tomorrow."

Chapter 26

From Malcolm's chair, it was four steps to the wall, a ninety-degree left turn, and seven steps to the bedroom, then eight steps back to his chair. If he measured correctly, walking the perimeter of this right triangle should carry him around the entire apartment without colliding into any furniture. His fascination with geometry before his blindness had preserved his sanity during his long hospitalization. But this triangle had a glitch. Walking the hypotenuse of the triangle should bring him back to his chair—if he took exactly 8.06 steps.

So how does one take six one hundredths of a step? Disregarding the math, he began his journey. To his surprise, the first trek around the course was successful, as were the second and third. But suddenly, his shin hit something hard. Most likely the table, or was it the chair? He shot his other leg forward to get around it. Then he felt a loss of balance. He felt dizzy. The therapist had warned him about this, how his semicircular canals needed time to adjust. But dammit, he had to walk. As he reached out to steady himself, memories of the explosion filled his head. Thrashing about with both hands, he felt airborne again. And then he fell.

First something hit his shoulder, and then his head. As he rolled onto the floor, his scarred face assured him it was wood. In silence, all he could picture was Jane's crumpled body, her gaping eyes and mouth. And now the certainty that her blood had covered his hands. Why did he allow Grace to burn his bloody trousers? Jane had been murdered. And he was an accomplice. He should have been home, comforting his cancer-riddled wife. Or better yet he should have died with her.

Yet he was entitled to live. It wasn't his fault. It was hers. That damn bitch, Whitney. With all his strength, he screamed, "Damn her! Damn her to hell! Why did you do this to me? I swear I'll kill you."

Suddenly, his door unlocked and swooshed open, and his nurse shouted, "Mr. Reinhardt, are you all right? Let me help you up."

As she lifted him to his knees, he screeched, "Where's my sister?"

"She's coming, sir. Any minute now."

As the nurse hauled him back to his chair, he rubbed his ribs with a clawed hand.

Plopping him into the recliner, she said, "There. How's that, sir?"

"I want Grace. Where is she?"

"Any second, sir. She always comes about this—"

As if his ranting had transported her into the room, he heard Grace say, "Malcolm, what happened?"

The nurse answered, "A nasty fall. But I think he's all right."

As Grace clutched his hands, more in an effort to silence him than to provide comfort, she said, "Are you hurt?"

"Just my pride, I fear. I felt dizzy and fell. I couldn't stop thinking about what she did to me."

Grace patted his hand and then said, "Nurse, thanks for your help. But I think he's fine now."

As the nurse left and closed the door, Grace loosened her grip and said, "You mean Whitney, of course?"

"Damn right. We need to finish her. Where the hell is that Inspector Stuhl and the real FBI guy, Jack Monihan? I'm beginning to think that Stuhl and his gut feelings are useless. Let's drag his ass in and find out what he's doing."

"I thought you might want to see him, so I've already asked that he meet us today. As a crime victim, you have the right to know the investigation's status."

Spreading his favorite blanket over his legs and tucking the edges inward, she said, "Now, Malcolm, I do have some disappointing news."

"What the hell now?"

"My man Felix reports we've apparently lost connection to Whitney's phone and computer."

"How'd that happen?"

"He believes either she or Falcone discovered the tap. The last download was her meeting with your former client, that crazy broad, Cindy Franklin."

"What do you mean former?"

"That's the other news. This morning's paper reports her suicide. Seems she stood on the tracks trying to stop a train."

Extricating his hands from beneath the blanket, he said, "Now how are we going to prove that dead bitch was connected to Whitney, the attack on me, the house explosion, and probably the attack on Mike Peller?"

"That's what I hope we can learn from Stuhl. We need to know the depth of Franklin's involvement."

Scratching an island of crusty scar on his scalp, he said, "My memory is getting a little better each day. I believe that Franklin worked for or had a connection with Congressman Rye. She was a hot babe back then. We might need to reach out to the former congressman and pump him for info."

"Well, be careful. Remember, the congressman was not pleased about losing the trial that ultimately led to his censure."

"Yeah, I recall. But I think he knows the evidence against him was overwhelming. Plus we still have some business deals in common. I think he'll be all right. Besides, remember his favorite saying: 'The enemy of my enemy is my friend.'"

There was a knock on the door, and Malcolm heard his nurse say, "There's an Inspector Jeffrey Stuhl downstairs. He wants to see you. Is that a problem? Should I bring him up?"

Malcolm hissed back, "There's no problem for me, but maybe there is for him. Send him up, now!"

When Stuhl entered the room, Grace and Malcolm were surprised to learn that he had FBI Special Agent Jack Monihan in tow. As if he had organized this meeting himself, Stuhl said, "I believe you will be more comfortable if we sit at the kitchen table."

Caught off guard, Malcolm answered, "Yes, sir."

As they sat down, Malcolm fidgeted on the hard, straight-backed wooden chair. Its hardness was the main reason he ate most of his meals in the recliner. Listening to Stuhl pluck folders from what sounded like a leather bag, he wondered where and why he had lost his intimidating style. Stuhl should be addressing *him* as sir, cowering before his wealth and power. And somehow the power structure was reversed.

Next he heard a series of clicks and taps of metal against the tabletop. "I can never get this portable recorder to work," Stuhl muttered to Monihan.

"Are you recording this meeting?" Grace asked.

"Yes." Stuhl responded. "Is there a problem? As attorneys, you both know you needn't speak to us, and if you don't wish to, we will leave."

Malcolm, as if freshly fueled, fired back, "Inspector, we don't need to be lectured on the law. We are the ones who requested this meeting to learn what the hell is going on with your investigation. That is, if I can call what you're doing an investigation." Turning in the direction of Agent Monihan, he added, "Although you are always welcome here, I'm uncertain as to your purpose."

Stuhl, still retaining command, said, "There. I've got the recorder working. Let's begin. I'm Inspector Jeffrey Stuhl. Present with me is FBI Special Agent Jack Monihan. We are meeting with Malcolm and Grace Reinhardt. Our purpose is to clarify new facts pertinent to the grand jury subpoena targeting Dr. Susan Whitney and Dr. Ray Dreskin.

"Mr. Reinhardt, are you familiar with the facts surrounding a Ms. Cindy Franklin's suicide last night?"

"No."

"Was she a former client of yours in a medical malpractice case against Dr. Ray Dreskin?"

"Yes."

"Was there anything unusual about her case or about this woman?"

"Her professional relationship is protected by attorney–client privilege."

In the pause, Malcolm detected the shift in the balance of power. The shift became seismic when Stuhl said, "Mr. Reinhardt, there's no need to be so legal and to respond in one-word answers. There are new developments in this investigation, and we wish to clarify certain facts. We're here to help you."

Malcolm said, "Inspector Stuhl, did you ever meet Ms. Cindy Franklin?"

"No. Never."

As if Stuhl had lost his footing, he cleared his throat and said, "You know,

I'm on this special FBI task force because of my experience with the Capitol Police. The university tasks me with solving complex financial crimes."

Grace interjected, "Yes, we know that. It's written boldly on your bright red business card."

Stuhl took an audible deep breath. "I solved the case against Professor Selnerhoff. You must have heard of it."

"Not in California," Grace said.

Unperturbed, Stuhl continued, "He was a university professor that concocted an elaborate financial scheme to shift federal grant dollars to his personal accounts. He fancied himself a real mathematician. But due to my strong gut feelings and wide experience solving federal crimes, I followed the money and solved it. He was indicted and sentenced to a five-year prison term."

Grace said, "The university must be proud of you."

"Indeed," he answered.

Seizing the opportunity to strike, Malcolm said, "That vignette was exhilarating. But how does it solve the explosion of my home, my permanent deformity, and the destruction of my life? Have you solved that yet? Or doesn't my case recapture your past fame and glory of imprisoning Professor Selnerhoff?"

Although he was blind, Malcolm was certain he felt the burn from Stuhl's stare through his scar. Pontificating fools such as him were so vulnerable on the witness stand. And the best part was they were too proud to be embarrassed. Returning to their tiny university pond, they glorified in solving dorm-room thefts, obscene student text messages, and missed stop signs in campus parking lots.

Malcolm heard Stuhl yank out another folder, and then growled, "Mr. Reinhardt, how is your relationship with former congressman Rye?"

"Good. I consider him a friend."

"Do you have a business relationship with him?"

"Yes. We invested in some property together many years ago."

Malcolm heard the tap of a pencil against a pad. Then Stuhl said, "I see. And where is this property located?"

"They're various parcels of farmland in central and western New York. We both wanted to support grape farmers that make ice wine. And also perhaps build our summer retirement homes there."

"Do you stay in close contact with former congressman Rye?"

"Not really close."

"I see. Would that have anything to do with your acrimonious departure after the loss of his judicial case?"

"No."

For the first time, Agent Monihan spoke. "Are there annual financial records for these property investments?"

"Yes, of course."

"And as the attorney of record for the land purchases, are you also responsible for maintaining those financial records?"

"No. Our accountants handle those matters. They've done so for years."

Grace acted as if she suspected these questions were entering stormy waters, so she said, "This sounds like a fishing trip, gentlemen, we still have the question of who is responsible for the physical torture of my brother. If you're interested in these ancient property records, I suggest you file the appropriate court documents to obtain them. Then we will gladly supply them. Until then, if you have nothing to inform us about, this meeting is ended."

In a silky tone, Stuhl said, "Ms. Reinhardt, I understand your frustration. And yes, we are actively investigating the prime targets of this grand jury subpoena. I have a strong gut feeling about this case, just like the feeling that led to my conviction of Professor Selnerhoff. I follow my gut and track the money."

Stuhl asked again, "Are you certain you're unfamiliar with my indictment of Professor Selnerhoff? The whole case was on the AP wire services."

"No, I didn't see it in the *LA Times*," Grace jeered. "And I must have missed it on the CNN nightly news."

Hearing the door close and Grace locking it, Malcolm said, "Is he a pompous asshole or what?"

"He's definitely a legend in his own mind. I don't trust his competence. Plus could you smell him? He stinks to boot."

Chapter 27

At seven o'clock on the morning following Cindy Franklin's suicide, Susan was dressed and seated upright in her bed, holding Andy's private cell phone in her hand. As expected, it rang. Before the ringtones of "Canterbury Bells" ended, she answered and heard Andy say, "Are you OK?"

"Yes, but I hardly slept. I feel so bad. I shouldn't have left her the way I did."

"Sue, it's not your fault. My men were at her house shortly after we spoke. The woman was gone."

"I just wish it had ended differently."

Adopting his legal voice, he said, "There are some new developments in your case that change several assumed facts."

"Oh brother, just what I need for today."

"Can you get to the office right away?" he said, disregarding her plea.

"I'm on my way. Been showered and dressed since six a.m."

Entering his office, she found two different boxes on his desk, one smaller than the other. "More spy stuff?" she asked.

"Not really, but sort of." Opening the smaller one, he handed her a new iPhone. Removing the lid on the larger box, he extracted a MacBook Air laptop. Then he said, "The security team wasn't comfortable returning your old equipment. The viruses were too deeply entrenched. It's safer this way. Plus I need my cell phone." He grinned broadly. "You know, in case my many girlfriends call."

Returning his phone, she said, "Yeah, I wondered why I got all those sexy calls after midnight." She dropped into her customary chair. "Andy, I can't be taking all these gifts from—"

"Forget it. It's a business expense. I can't risk another intrusion into our conversations. So let's get down to business."

"I know that tone. There's a problem."

"Not necessarily a problem for you. Last night, the reason we couldn't chat is because the federal prosecutor asked to meet with me off the record."

"What does that mean?"

"Remember I told you that ATF had assumed primary lead for investigating the Reinhardt house explosion?"

"Yes, I do."

Opening a folder on his desk, he said, "The Bureau of Alcohol, Tobacco, Firearms and Explosives has a national lab called the Fire Research Laboratory. They have sophisticated forensic tools to analyze fires and explosions. The Reinhardt home, or what remained of it, was exhaustively studied. These are the key findings." He put his half-frame reading glasses on. "When Malcolm was catapulted through the patio glass, his loafers traveled a few feet farther. Those shoes had two interesting details. The tip of the right toe, in the crease between the sole and the leather upper, contained blood traces."

He paused to lift another sheet of the report. "The heel of the left shoe was even more interesting. The rubber heel had been manufactured with a corrugated grooved pattern. These creases were found to contain a significant quantity of blood, and due to the heat of the explosion, the uppermost rubber congealed and formed small caverns that preserved the captured blood."

He gazed up at her. "The end result is that the lab did a DNA match and determined the blood was from Jane Reinhardt."

Her mouth fell open, and Susan said, "Does that mean Mrs. Reinhardt was dead before the explosion occurred?"

"Exactly. But of greater interest is that Malcolm had dropped down on his right knee to examine her body, thereby dipping the toe of his right shoe into her blood. And in order to drop to his right knee, he used his left leg to stabilize himself, and that leg had its shoe heel braced in a larger quantity of blood."

"So did Reinhardt kill her?"

"We don't have direct evidence of that, but we know that when Reinhardt was discharged from the hospital, his tattered clothes were given to the family in a bag. That bag included trousers, but now the Feds can't find them."

"What's the significance there?" she asked.

With a grin, Andy responded, "Grace Reinhardt had the bag of clothing, but the pants were missing. Given the shoe evidence, the right knee area of the pants should have bloodstains. So where are those trousers?"

"Are we suggesting that the holier-than-thou Reinhardt duo tampered with evidence?"

"It's a speculation."

Rustling through more papers in the report, Andy said, "But the most complex piece of forensic evidence is this. The fire lab analyzed two pieces of the patio door glass. One piece had a partial bloody palm print that matches Malcolm. But the second piece, which is confirmed to have come from the glass adjacent to the patio door handle, has a bloody print from a left fourth finger. And that print doesn't match Malcolm, his sister, or Jane."

Susan asked, "Are we saying those are the killer's prints?"

Reorganizing the splayed papers on his desk, he said, "Could be a killer, a houseguest, a repairman, or a host of characters."

She gave a deep sigh. "So is that print a red herring? A piece of unfounded data useless to us?"

"Not so fast, Dr. Part-Time Lawyer. That print matches another one found on a microswitch embedded in the wall switch that Malcolm flipped and that ignited the blast."

"What the hell? I thought Stuhl and the cops concluded it was a loose wire in the switch?"

With a broad smile, Andy folded his hands. "And now we come to the most interesting speculation, suggested by forensic facts. The microswitch is a wireless remote-control device. It was installed by someone. But why?"

Unfolding his hands to tap the desk, he continued, "Because, if Malcolm didn't flip the wall switch to trigger the explosion, then someone was probably outside, prepared to commit the act." He tapped the desk again, only much harder. "This strongly suggests a coordinated plot, not a depressed cancer patient intent on suicide."

"So why did the prosecutor give you this report?"

"The prosecutor is a very hard-nosed lawyer, but he's fair. This report is exculpatory evidence."

"By the way, I hear that word a lot on TV, but what exactly does it mean?"

Leaning back in his chair, Andy said, "It comes from the Latin word *exculpatus*, which means to free of guilt. Exculpatory evidence is evidence that doesn't help the prosecutor convict you of a crime. But it might free you of blame or guilt. By law, even though such evidence is unintended or unexpected from the prosecutor's point of view, it must be turned over to the defense side."

She nodded. "I see. So how does this all add up for me?"

"At this point it means that, regarding the home explosion, it would hard to convict you. Although both you and Dreskin could have motive, the setting of a microswitch and a gas explosion is atypical doctor behavior. Plus you were working that entire night. However, the assault in the hospital is a different story. Motive, ability, and time of the event support suspicion of both of you."

"What about the fingerprint thing? Are they pursuing that?"

Andy removed his reading glasses. "They are. Matter of fact, they're also investigating Cindy Franklin's computer. From what I understand, it was seriously infected with a ton of viruses, but they confirm the screen name you saw, Larpa369."

"Cindy told me there was an online lover she chatted with. And that he provided her with the mercury capsules I showed you."

"Yes, you did. Which, by the way, gets us out of the problem of defending your rummaging through her house. The only problem is they didn't find any drugs in her house except legal meds ordered by Dr. Dreskin." Andy scanned his watch. "I have another appointment, but there is this other concern. It appears the ATF boys are not too impressed with Inspector Stuhl. Might be interagency rivalry. Sort of like how the FBI sees themselves as smarter than the Secret Service, or the US Marshals as better than the small-time city cops. Apparently Stuhl was a bit upset about these findings. They don't support his gut feelings."

"You know what I think of him."

"Be that as it may, there's more to this case than two doctors pissed off at a malpractice lawyer."

Chapter 28

Malcolm's private aide had just removed his breakfast tray when Grace entered his living area. Listening to the sound of papers spreading across the table in front of him, he wondered why she hadn't spoken a word. So he said, "Good morning to you also. Seems you're preoccupied. What's wrong?"

"I'm sorry, Malcolm, there's a couple new twists to our perfect plan."

"Now what?"

He felt her drop onto the couch next to him. "There are two problems," she said. "But let me start by saying how happy I am to watch your improvement each day."

"OK, don't butter me up. Just tell me—what are the two problems?"

"I just received some court documents, which I brought with me. They've ordered an exhumation of Jane's body."

Gasping as if the air were rationed, he exclaimed, "What the hell for?"

"The ATF and the FBI believe, based on forensic evidence, that Jane's death wasn't a suicide. They've located the shoes you were wearing that night. There was blood on them, and testing confirms it was Jane's."

Regaining his composure, like he used to do during a difficult trial, he said, "And I suppose they're wondering about my missing trousers."

Following a distinct pause, she said in a near whisper, "Yes. I had to give them the bag of your clothes. That is a problem that I have several ideas on how to solve."

Responding to her like he would to a first-year law student, he said, "I hope you do. I'll be interested to hear your theories."

She cleared her voice. "Both the ATF and Agent Monihan are concerned about the forensic evidence, which exposed an unknown trace of blood on a section of patio glass." Before he could cross-examine her, she said, "They haven't run that blood through all their databases. But so far there's no match."

He shook his head, wishing he could stand and pace like he used to do in the courtroom. "I should have known this would come back to bite us in the ass. When I first regained consciousness, only then did I recall her blood on my hands. I should have reported it. That would have triggered a murder investigation and kept us on offense rather than defense."

He heard her shuffle some papers as she said, "In examining the court order to exhume, I see it's based on the blood findings as well as the previous discovery of a wireless microswitch in the kitchen light switch."

"So someone got into the house, killed Jane, and then planted an ignition switch as a backup."

She said, "Yes. You always could come to a conclusion faster than me."

"All right. You stated there were two problems. What's the other?"

"The other is a bit more convoluted. It deals with the board of directors from the hospital and university. As you recall, their chairman, Richard Cambridge, had met with me a couple times before."

Nodding, Malcolm said, "Yes, to buy us off and stop us from suing them into bankruptcy."

"When I first discussed this with you, you were in the early stages of healing. Let me fill you in on the details and the urgent meeting they demanded I attend last night. The board chairman is a wealthy investment broker and major landowner in central and western New York."

"Yeah, I know the name. Probably shook his hand several times at Congressman Rye's many fundraisers. He's a Southern boy who moved to New York, probably with the intent to buy most of our vacant land."

Grace continued, "The vice-chairwoman of both the hospital and university boards is Annalee Jackson. She is a strong-willed and opinionated leader who has major influence on both the university and hospital. Her husband's family owns a major bourbon distillery in Kentucky. And as you would expect, both are major donors to the hospital and universities. Anyway, she and Cambridge demanded we meet last night at her home."

"Well, what did they want?"

As she paused to clear her throat, he could feel her discomfort as she said, "They sense the spotlight is on us and its intensity will only brighten. So they suggested that they were too generous in their previous financial offer to us. They also discussed how our current status might hamper the hospital's application for a comprehensive cancer center."

"Those bastards. I knew they'd run the first chance they could. Somehow I smell Whitney as the root cause of this."

"How do you think Whitney did that?"

"That Dreskin character and she might have corralled the doctors to threaten the board with moving their patients to another hospital. Believe me, Grace, doctors are as vicious as any labor leader."

Grace said, "Perhaps she's playing the gender card. How the administration mistreats women. OK, we need to increase our pressure, Malcolm. What do you suggest?"

"First off, we need to get Henry Taylor appointed as the executive vice president for health affairs. He's the most punctilious person I know. He'll never allow any deviation from his code of rules and regulations. And most importantly, he can be bought. We just have to be certain we're the highest bidder."

"I agree, brother. How do we do it?"

"As I told you, we need to meet with Congressman Rye ASAP. He's no longer in government, but like every senior elected official who leaves office, whether in scandal or glory, he can get a job with the medical insurance industry. As a matter of fact, those leaving in scandal are more desirable. Why? Because their buyers are certain they now own slaves without a soul."

"If that's true, Malcolm—if Congressman Rye is enslaved to his new master—why would he help us?"

"Ah, Grace, therein lies the paradox. The congressman may have new masters, but he is woefully linked with durable chains to his past lords."

Chapter 29

It was almost a week since Susan had met with Andy. She was curious and impatient to learn if he had any new developments. Plus, she needed his advice on the offer from the board of directors to buy her company.

She was brushing her hair when her cell phone rang. Racing to it and expecting it was Andy, she didn't notice the caller ID when she said, "Hello." But there was only silence. Scanning the screen, she saw it was an unidentified number. Robocall. Her finger was a mere inch away from ending the call when she heard, "Hello, Susan."

The voice was muffled, as if the caller had a cold. Then the man said, "I know who you are. I watch you all the time. Do you know who I am?"

"Are you a new telemarketer? Well, say 'goodbye.'"

She paused just long enough to assuage her curiosity. That was a mistake. It gave the man a chance to say, "Oh, you'll get to know me more. I know what you did to Malcolm Reinhardt. And I can prove it. I'm your grim reaper, scheduled to pay you back." His voice echoed like it was coming from a well. "Your sweet ass is mine."

And then, as swiftly as it had started, the call ended. She stared at her phone, and her hand began to tremble. She wanted to call Andy, but she feared the phone had a bug. Plodding her way back to the bathroom, she picked up her hairbrush and gazed into the mirror. The reflected image seemed to have aged a decade since she awoke. Why was this happening? Who was he? Although the voice sounded artificially masked, there was something familiar. But who, or what, was behind it? With one sweep of the brush through her hair, she strode to the closet and grabbed her coat, intending to drive straight to Andy's office.

As soon as Susan entered his office, Andy's assistant recognized her level of anxiety and said, "He does have a full schedule this morning, but let me get you in."

She was seated on the edge of a waiting room chair when his assistant returned. "Let me bring you into a conference room," she said. "He'll be right with you."

She paced around the conference table and then stared out the window at the downtown buildings as people scurried about. She wondered who out there had called. When Andy entered the room, his expression confirmed that he saw her angst. Gesturing toward a chair, he said, "Sue, what's wrong?"

Taking a seat, she wrung her hands to control the shake and relayed her recent phone call.

Sighing, he said, "So do you think this voice is familiar to you?"

"I'm not sure, but something about it is. Andy, I'm so scared and confused. I'm uncertain about everything."

To her surprise, he said, "Just as I'm certain you will be confused about the recent call I received from Vice-Chairwoman Annalee Jackson." He grinned, perhaps to bring color to her face. "I was certain she wasn't calling for me to defend her for capital murder. Although anything is possible with a billionaire."

Unclasping her hands, Susan said, "That's what I wanted to come over and discuss with you. That is, before I got that phone call. I received an offer from Ms. Annalee Jackson, relayed to me by Ray Dreskin."

With a chiding tone, he said, "You got what kind of offer from Ms. Jackson and conveyed to you by Dreskin?" Before she could reply, he added, "Sue, you should have called me directly after Dr. Dreskin's visit."

"Andy, I just can't be continually imposing on you at all hours of the day," she said defensively. "I probably shouldn't have just barged in today."

Before her head dropped any lower, he said professionally, "Sue, Ms. Jackson instructed me clearly, as I'm certain she does all her helper monkeys, that she is the solution to your problems. Which are mounting legal bills. Naturally, she assumes your naivety impairs your comprehension. Hence the call to me to draft legal documents, which her legal counsel will make worthy for a court." With a facial expression matching his sarcasm, he said, "Did I accurately condense the message that Dr. Dreskin bumbled?"

As always, he made her laugh. "Not bad for an unworthy peon," she said.

"Seriously, though, what motives do you attach to Dreskin's actions?"

"I'm not sure. I was always suspicious of his smooth, oily approach, which began when he lied for me the day of Reinhardt's attack. But right now I'm more worried about this morning's phone call. Do we call the cops or what?"

"There's a possibility the call and the $3 million offer for your company are connected. I can't prove that now, but I'll investigate it. And yes, we will get you protection."

"Thanks, Andy. I'm so sorry to add these burdens onto your day."

"Forget that, Sue. Let's concentrate on solving this mystery. The major crimes in this entire mess are murder and a possible related suicide. Tomorrow is the planned exhumation of Jane Reinhardt's body. Her murder raises the question, Who did it, and why? We know from the forensic data that Malcolm was the primary target all along. The last concern, and frankly the most pressing issue for Inspector Stuhl, is your alleged theft of university services and misuse of grant funds you never received."

"Yeah, it figures that Jeffrey Stuhl would focus on that instead of who stole a bra from Victoria's Secret in the mall."

As Andy stood and began his thoughtful pacing, he said, "And why would the power broker of the board of directors reach out to me to initiate a deal to buy you? Although your charitable work is admirable, the timing and payout of three million is a mystery. There's something wrong with this entire picture."

Apparently frustrated by his own thoughts, Andy turned and said, "I'm going to demand a meeting with the prosecutor, now! Go home; I'll get back to you with security, as well as to tell you what I've learned."

Barely saying goodbye, he strode from the room. Alone in silence, Susan felt the caller's threats ooze down her spine. Like wounded prey, she began to tremble.

Chapter 30

It had been a week since Malcolm, accompanied by Grace, had left his apartment. As frightened as he was of being viewed by outside people, Grace was able to ameliorate his fears. The last outing, a visit to his plastic surgeon, Tom Cook, was painless. And other than hearing young ladies speaking medical chat, he assumed the waiting room was empty.

However, today was a very different trip. His outreach to former congressman Rye had been accepted, and their meeting would be at the congressman's home. Grace would escort him, but, per the congressman's request, she wouldn't participate in their meeting. To assuage his fear of being outside, Grace had replaced his former sports car with a Range Rover Velar SUV, fully equipped with plush leather seats that mimicked his recliner, FM radio with Bose sound system, and, most importantly, double-darkened windows. Wisely, Grace had also hired a private driver so that she could chat with Malcolm during the hour-long ride to Congressman Rye's home.

As they left for their visit, Malcolm was agitated, but listening to Debussy's "Clair de Lune," he relaxed in thought. Arriving at their destination, or, as Grace called it, the royal mansion, Malcolm was prepared. Grace guided him up the curved concrete steps, and the congressman opened the door before they could ring the bell. After his warm greeting, both their spirits brightened.

Spending several minutes in the adjoining tearoom off the main foyer, they made small talk, as old friends might do. But when the congressman's wife arrived, it was suggested that perhaps Grace might enjoy viewing the enclosed garden room featuring Mrs. Rye's state-award-winning collection of orchids.

As Grace departed, Congressman Rye helped his friend stroll to the library. Upon entering it, Malcolm detected a familiar scent of cigar smoke that recalled their many late-night meetings. Guiding Malcolm into his familiar, deeply padded leather chair, Rye said, "Malcolm, I'm sure you recall the business tycoons we hosted here and the great legislation we crafted."

Employing Rye's first name, which Malcolm never did in the presence of others, he said, "William, yes, I do. And I must say I miss it. More so in my present condition than ever before."

"As I miss you also, Malcolm. Yet it was hard for me to forgive our unfortunate separation."

"I'm aware of that. I did try my best to mount a successful defense for the charges that were conflated with public opinion that failed to recognize managed medical care as America's future."

As Rye lit a cigar, its aroma instantly filled the room. Then he said, "Perhaps in my rush to judgment, I focused my wrath on you rather than that bitch Sue Whitney. God curse her soul."

With a sigh of relief, Malcolm said, "Exactly my thoughts." Pointing a scarred, deformed right index finger to his former eye, he added, "I know she did this to me!"

"So how do we render justice, my old friend?"

"That's why I'm here. My entire case is clouded by a bungled investigation that caused a dysfunctional hospital board of directors to retract a settlement offer."

Following an audible puff on his cigar, Rye said, "Why has the board reneged on its offer?"

"They're confused and too focused on their super plans for an NCI-designated comprehensive cancer center."

"Is it possible, Malcolm, that you might have done something, perhaps inadvertently, to give the board cause?"

Sad that he wasn't holding a cigar, which would have permitted a long pause, he said, "I was sick, William. I nearly died. My memory was faulty. I didn't report the blood surrounding June's body."

"I see. So you agree it appears your wife was murdered? Who would want to do that?"

"I have no idea."

"I believe I've heard an Inspector Jeffrey Stuhl is the lead investigator in this case. How's he working out for you?"

"At first I thought he was great. Clearly focused on nailing the prime suspect, Whitney, and her supposed buddy Ray Dreskin. But since the ATF introduced all this forensic bullshit, it appears Stuhl has been marginalized. I think now he's way out of his league."

"Indeed, that's sad. We must stay focused on the true bitch. The one who caused us so much pain, so much difficulty. We must refocus our goals and work together, as once we did. Which recalls another matter."

"What's that, William?"

"As you know, you and I hold critical property in central and western New York."

"Yes, beautiful country in the Finger Lakes region."

"Correct, Malcolm. Beautiful place to grow grapes. But also a critical place to sow future health-care centers. And as you recall, we drew up very carefully worded contracts to protect our personal concerns. Contracts with binding nondisclosures. We agreed to those terms so that neither of us could ever disclose what property interests we had and where. This was particularly important to me as an elected official, and to you as an unconflicted officer of the court. But now, looking into our respective futures, wouldn't it be preferable if I bought out your half of the contract?"

Clearing his throat, which was irritated by smoke, Malcolm said, "But I always dreamed of building a peaceful and beautiful retirement home with a view of one of the Finger Lakes during the fall and winter grape harvest."

Raising his voice, Rye said, "Malcolm, with all due respect, you're fucking blind. Is not our most meaningful goal the pursuit of justice? Is that not your lawyer's oath? Should we not focus our actions on delivering justice? Would your future needs not be better served by cash and its power rather than past dreams?"

"William, all I have are past dreams. I'm a shell of a man, one who fully understands the jailhouse term 'dead man walking.' So I trust you understand I will get revenge on Whitney for both our benefits, but I just can't relinquish my property holdings."

Malcolm heard the congressman squash his cigar into the crystal ashtray. "I understand, Malcolm," he said. "Let us speak no further on this subject. Perhaps we should check on the ladies."

The congressman led Malcolm back to Grace. After a few perfunctory remarks on how they should all meet again, the Ryes escorted them to the door.

Once inside the steel cocoon of the Range Rover, Grace said, "So how did your meeting go?"

"Good, really good. I think we can rely on the congressman to refocus everyone on destroying Whitney."

Chapter 31

Two days after meeting with Andy, Susan still feared another threatening call. Marooned in her apartment with only her medical journals and a few novels, she spent her time catching up on unread interests. Andy, as expected, fulfilled his promise to request extra police coverage. The periodic police car parked in front of her apartment conveyed comfort. Whether their presence was because of her or the Greek deli across the street didn't matter. In fact, what would they do should she receive a call? Yet she was grateful, especially at night.

Curled up on the couch, dressed in a Buffalo Bills T-shirt above blue pajama bottoms, she studied the images for a new laparoscopic surgical tool. The hard knock on her door startled her. Instinctively, she bellowed out, "Who's there?"

"Deliveryman."

Stealthily treading to the double-bolted door, she peered through the wide-angle lens of the peephole. Observing only a thin middle-aged man dressed in a sweatshirt and a black baseball cap that covered his forehead, she demanded, "Where's the package from?"

She spied the man turn the long, narrow white box embellished with a red bow and ribbon on its side. He read the label and said, "Says Evergreen Florists."

Stepping backward, she thought either Andy or Dreskin must have sent them. So she said firmly, "Just leave the box in front of the door." She was prepared to tell him to beat it should he demand a signature. When she peered through the peephole again, he was gone.

Unlocking the door, she braced her foot against it and cracked it ajar. No one was in sight. The package was on the floor. She seized the box with one hand and dragged it in. The bow and ribbons appeared professionally tied, and the bright red-and-yellow mailing label displayed the florist's name and address. Picking it up with both hands, she gently shook it. It was light enough for flowers, and it sounded stuffed with paper. Mentally chiding herself for being such a wimp, she carried it into her bedroom. She thought to get dressed first, but after placing the box on the bed, her curiosity prevailed, and she untied the ribbon to remove the cover.

As she expected, she saw roses. A dozen, it appeared. Brilliant, long-stemmed red and yellow roses paired in an unusual pattern of alternating red and yellow flowers. As their pleasant aroma scented the air, she lay across the bed to smell them closer. In that position, she spotted a small white envelope slipping toward the bottom of the box. Anxious to learn the sender, she reached into the box and grasped the flowers with one hand while the other seized the envelope.

Suddenly, both her left hand and right forearm were skewered with unbearable pain. As she yanked both arms high into the air above her prone body, two striped snakes followed. Rolling away, she tangled herself into the sheets, which covered the snake on her right arm. Screaming in pain, she watched the other snake, inches from her face, chew her left hand. Rolling backward off the bed with a blanket caught between her legs, she howled loudly enough that surely God must have heard.

Miraculously, the snake on her right arm slithered away beneath the bedsheets. Wildly shaking her left arm, she clutched the snake's body with her right hand and yanked it with all her might. Tearing her skin, the snake dropped away to carry her flesh under the bed.

Spotting her phone on the nightstand, she grasped it with her right hand and staggered to the front door. As blood oozed down her arm, she unlocked the door and fell to her knees in the empty hallway. Pulling the door shut, she screamed for help. As her vision narrowed and her airway began to close, she touched the phone icon. Tapping 911, she passed into darkness.

Chapter 32

Andy was at his desk reviewing a plausible defense for an upcoming trial when his assistant buzzed him that the federal prosecutor was holding on line two. Picking up, Andy said, "Good morning, Louis. What's up?"

"Andy, I have bad news. Sue Whitney is in Monroe General's ICU. Somehow this morning she was bitten by two venomous coral snakes. I understand that Dr. Harrison is the lead doctor in her care." As the line remained silent, he added, "I'm sorry, Andy, but I wanted to let you know first."

With a knot in his throat, Andy said, "How did it happen?"

"We don't have the particulars, but apparently she received some flower package. The police are in her apartment now. The snakes have been caught and confirmed venomous. Because of the other complexities, the FBI will soon be on the scene."

Struggling to stay focused, he said, "Thanks, Louis. Let me know if you hear more."

He left his office and passed his assistant's desk. "I'll be at the hospital," he said. "Call me only for emergencies."

He arrived at the hospital and convinced the staff that, although he wasn't a relative, he needed to see Susan Whitney. A nurse guided him through the maze of corridors to the small waiting area. As he sat on a plastic seat supported by four metal spindles, he prayed as hard as he could.

After several minutes, the door labeled Staff Only opened, and a gray-haired doctor wearing a blue surgical scrub shirt over baggy blue pants appeared. Approaching Andy, he said, "Mr. Falcone?"

He stood. "Yes, Doctor, how is she?"

The doctor still held onto Andy's arm after a firm handshake. "Come with me," he said. They trekked down more corridors. "I'm Dr. Harrison. May I call you Andy? Sue has spoken so often about you; I believe we might be friends."

"Yes, of course. And she considers you her primary mentor and friend."

Passing through a series of automatic doors, they entered a large circular room whose perimeter was studded with glass doors that opened into rooms filled with computer monitors that flashed ever-changing numbers, graphs, and wave patterns. Crowding the monitors were steel posts that stacked several infusion pumps above each other. Each pump further connected to clear plastic bags filled with multicolored liquids. Some rooms had what Andy recognized as a breathing machine that projected large tubes connected to a patient's face or throat. Perhaps most startling was the cacophony of sounds—rhythmical sounds for each puff of air, the steady sharp hiss of suction pumps, all interrupted by bells, buzzers, and melodic rings of steady heartbeats.

As he scanned the room, trying to understand its coordination, he gazed upon the central station, where nurses were focused on more computer monitors. These nurses wore shirts of a color different than those of the nurses rushing in and out of patient rooms. It reminded him of an aircraft carrier's flight deck, with each shirt color identifying a person's specialized skills.

Suddenly, Dr. Harrison stopped in front of a door tagged with a white card labeled Susan Whitney. As Andy stared through the glass, he fought back tears, seeing all the machines surrounding her bed. Most notable to him were the two large tubes merging into one tube that curved away from her mouth. Above her mouth, a smaller tube, which was fixed to her nose with strips of white tape that covered her cheekbones, cascaded to a canister adjacent to the bed.

Dr. Harrison recognized his shock and said, "It will be touch-and-go for a few days. She took a sizable venom dose. So we've induced a coma to allow the mechanical ventilator to breathe for her. Coral snake venom is a neurotoxin that targets the respiratory muscles. I took her to surgery on arrival to address the tissue wound on her left hand."

Andy leaned against the door frame with his back to Susan. "Will she make it?"

"We're doing everything possible to assure that she does. But we'd feel better if we had the antivenom."

"Well, what the hell? Why don't you have it? Besides, I thought coral snake bites weren't fatal."

Sighing, Dr. Harrison said, "That's true, most bites are not. But we reviewed the pictures sent to us by the cops who caught the snakes. Those colorful stripes on the body tell a story that supports an old wife's tale. It depends on the order of stripes. The rhyme goes, 'Red touch yellow, kill a fellow, red touch black, friend of Jack.' Her bites were from a rarely seen coral snake, and unfortunately, the stripes were red abutted to yellow."

"So what's the problem with getting antivenom?"

Dr. Harrison shook his head. "If Sue recovers, I'm certain this will be her next blog post on SpotofHope.com. Coral snake antivenom was manufactured by Pfizer, which ceased its production in 2012. Technically the antivenom expired in 2008, but each year the FDA extends the expiration date by one year. Basically, Pfizer feels that for the estimated fifteen to twenty-five venomous coral snake bites per year, it's not worth the $5–10 million to research a new synthetic antivenom."

Spotting the fire that burned inside Dr. Harrison's blue eyes, Andy said, "What the hell is that?"

"That's the medical insurance industry's support of the pharmaceutical complex. For Pfizer to produce blue pills that harden an old man's stiffy, that justifies research and production. But a cure for appendiceal cancer, which impacts only one in four million Americans per year? Not worth it. But over that same year, the CEO enjoys a $27.9 million salary." Then Dr. Harrison took Andy's arm. "Let's go in and see her."

Andy gently moved closer to her bed, feeling increasingly helpless. As he gazed at her face, thoughts of their past good years exploded in his head. What had happened? Was he at fault? And if she awakened, would he let her crumble due to an incomplete legal defense? Reaching out, he touched her left forearm above the bandages.

Dr. Harrison said, "Why don't you sit here for a few minutes? We don't normally permit visitors inside the ICU, but this might be an exception." Patting Andy's shoulder, he left the room.

As Andy pulled a plastic chair to the foot of the bed, he gazed around the area and observed nurses scurrying in various directions. Focusing on Susan's face, he began to cry.

Chapter 33

Grace read the daily news to Malcolm each morning, but the article covering the Susan Whitney attack was incomplete. As Malcolm awaited his sister's arrival, he was hopeful that her meeting with the federal prosecutor and Inspector Stuhl this morning would alleviate his concerns.

When Grace entered his room, he could tell by her brisk footsteps that his worries had been addressed. Dropping into a seat next to him, she gently shook his wrist and said, "I think you'll be happy with this news. Plus we'll need to recalculate our position with that two-faced board of directors."

After an audible deep breath, she said, "As you know, Whitney was attacked, but the news didn't say who, or should I say what, attacked her." Malcolm sensed she could barely stifle her giddiness. "Two freaking poisonous coral snakes, wrapped in a bed of roses." Breaking into laughter, she shook his wrist more firmly. "How about that, baby!"

Although it was still painful to move his jaw, he guffawed. "I told you we could count on Congressman Rye. When he promises to take care of matters, he's a man of his word. So how's the bitch doing now?"

"Well, she's been in ICU for two days. The best part is they haven't located any antivenom. So she's in a coma while machines do her breathing. They're keeping her alive and hoping the venom burns away, I guess."

"I suffered a hell of a lot more. Maybe now she'll understand payback. Although, goddamn, I wonder how Rye thought that vengeance up and got someone to pull it off?"

"The cops have no idea who did it. However, the other news is the results of Jane's second autopsy."

"Now that's important," he said.

"Basically the cops are dealing with the same problem we deal with in every medical malpractice case: expert witnesses disagree. The original pathologist and now the new one have reached different conclusions."

Laughing even louder, he said, "And if we had a dozen of them, we'd have thirteen different opinions. So what's the new guy opining?"

"He states Jane was stabbed with a long thin blade in the right neck. The knife tip was pointed downward to the chest and pierced several big arteries and ultimately the heart. He concludes death was a homicide, and the stab wound accounts for the voluminous blood found at the scene."

"OK. So how about the first pathologist—who, by the way, is a hometown university boy, working regularly with the prosecutor's office every week, and whom they count on for speedy prosecution of all their cases—what does he have to say after this out-of-towner just kicked his ass?"

Giggling, she said, "Malcolm, you're such a cynic, but you're usually right. He vociferously defended his opinion by stating that the explosion ripped Jane's body apart. That the shock and trauma tore open her organs. Furthermore, Jane's embedded chemotherapy port was located in her right chest and connected to her heart. So to claim that a knife wound caused the bleeding, he said, disregards the fact that there was tissue damage to her right neck and chest from when the chemo port burst during the explosion. Also, he stated that the reported bloodstains on the glass and your clothing required liquid not coagulated blood. And since the confirmed time of death and your arrival home are within minutes of each other, her blood must have been in a liquid and not a coagulated state. The doctor ended his report by concluding the blood spatter is chaotic and invalidates the second doctor's conclusions."

"Just what I would expect."

"Oh, and by the way, Inspector Stuhl may not be as dumb as we thought. He now, more strongly than ever, expounds his gut feelings that Whitney and Dreskin, working together with an undiscovered colleague, committed all these acts on you."

Malcolm, now gratified, leaned back in his recliner. "Let us now plan how to manipulate the board of directors. I suggest you immediately invite both Chairman Cambridge and his snarky-mouthed vice-chairperson, Annalee Jackson, to a sit-down."

"I agree; I'll do it."

"It's time we show them who's in control and our definition of justice. First off, their so-called generous offer for settlement has been doubled by me. To ensure their obedience and to thwart any future desires to impugn my reputation, we shall demand that you be given a seat on their board. Should they find this too bitter a pill to swallow, then we shall pursue litigation by public trial. Let them visualize a jury concluding that my injuries resulted from some misdoing on their part. Let them muse over the status of their cancer center's application amid devastating public opinion."

He could almost see her broad smile as she said, "God, I'm going to enjoying screwing that bitch Whitney and that pompous Annalee Jackson, born in wealth but soon to crawl into infamy."

Chapter 34

Directly after receiving a call from Dr. Harrison informing him that Susan was awake and breathing on her own, Andy canceled his next appointment and sped to the hospital. Once there, he was thrilled to learn she was no longer in the ICU. Discovering her new room number and floor, he nearly levitated to it.

Entering her room, he threw all legal professionalism aside and hugged her so firmly he wondered if it was medically contraindicated. Dr. Harrison, entering the room slightly behind him, said, "Figured you didn't see me when you flew by. But it's good to see you hugging my favorite patient. Her latest test results are looking fine." He wagged a finger at Susan. "She can go home tomorrow, if she can stay away from exotic snakes and insurance company CEOs."

Confirming her improved health, Susan said, "Aren't they both snakes?"

Dr. Harrison gave her a pleading gaze. "Andy, is there any way you can keep her out of trouble?"

"Doctor, I promise I'll try."

Turning to leave, he gazed back and said with a broad grin, "Why don't you guys visit a little longer. But remember, this is a hospital. All sorts of people drop in unannounced."

Andy sat on the edge of her bed, still holding her unbandaged right hand. "So how do you feel?"

"I felt nothing after passing out in the hallway. It wasn't until last night when I woke up that I felt anything. I now understand what patients go through, trying to stay calm while a machine does all their breathing. But this morning, after they removed the breathing tube, I felt weak but a whole lot better."

Squeezing her hand, he said, "Thank God."

She sat up in bed as Andy adjusted her pillows. "So what's new in my case?"

Fluffing the pillows allowed him more time to organize an answer. At last he proffered, "Nothing critical, and I don't think this is a good time to talk about legal stuff. You need to rest and heal."

With a piercing gaze, she said, "I've been asleep for two days, so don't patronize me. Besides, I can tell when you're hiding something. So tell me. I'd rather learn the problems now than imagine the worst."

He shook his head. "Gods, Sue, can't even two poisonous snakes slow you down? Take it easy. Don't bite my head off."

"Andy, I'm sorry. But I just need to know my status."

"Sue, let's give it a rest. In my judgment, this isn't the time or the place."

Leaning forward off the pillows, she said, "You're my lawyer, I'm the client, and—"

The door swooshed open, and two young nurses entered, one in a red shirt and the other in a white one. "Good morning, Dr. Whitney," the nurse in red said. "We need to get your morning blood tests and vitals." Both moved with deliberate alacrity as they pulled their respective mobile carts behind them and began their organized data collection.

Andy leaped off the bed and stood in a corner, wondering if her blood pressure would blow a fuse or set off an alarm. Watching her blood fill a tube, he hoped her anger would drain too.

When the nurses had completed their tasks, the white-clad nurse said, "Your vitals look great." She and the nurse in red departed as quickly as they'd entered.

"Look, Sue, let's not fight about this," Andy said. "I don't think we should discuss this any further today."

Unfazed, she continued, "As I was saying, I'm the client, you're my lawyer. Professionally, you're obligated to answer my questions and tell me my exact legal status. So I demand to know…or else."

"Or else what, you'll get another lawyer?" He pulled up a chair at the foot of her bed and said, "OK, here's the latest report, up to the minute." He took a deep breath to regain his legal composure. "The second autopsy performed on Mrs. Reinhardt is inconclusive. The second pathologist concludes she was murdered prior to the explosion, but his opinion is strongly rebutted by the university pathologist, who concludes her blood splatter and ruptured organs were due solely to the trauma of the explosion."

"So that's good news for my case, right?"

"Bluntly, it means the official cause of death will remain suicide. But her death is a serious secondary crime in the allegations that you and Dr. Dreskin intended to kill Malcolm Reinhardt. And by the way, the lead investigator, Jeffrey Stuhl, strongly insists this was his gut feeling all along."

Nearly bouncing in her bed, she said, "Goddamn, when are they going to give him a scooter and a walkie-talkie and send him to a mall?"

"Not today, Sue."

"So is there more? I don't think this is what you wanted to hold back from me."

He took an extra-deep breath and realized that her medications over the past several days had left her unsettled. "Yes, you're correct. There's more. The FBI, with the assistance of a couple other federal agencies, decrypted the badly damaged and infected hard drive of Cindy Franklin. They recovered numerous exchanges between her and Larpa369. There is no doubt he poisoned her with mercury in tainted capsules." Hesitating for several seconds, he dropped his head and said, "They also identified his computer's IP address and traced it to a Lawrence Parnell. Does that name ring a bell?"

Susan dropped back against her bunched pillows. "Yes. He's a dentist with a severe drug addiction. Other counselors and I worked with him through Spot of Hope."

"Correct. Currently, he has outstanding warrants, along with these new ones. Since there are federal implications in this case, the US Marshals are out to apprehend him. Last night, they raided his run-down apartment in Troy, New York. They didn't catch him. However, his computer was seized and found to have compromising photos of you on it. In addition, there are message exchanges in which he uses the screen name Larpa369 and supposedly claims you and he had drug interactions."

"Holy shit, Andy, what's going on?"

Waving his hands to preclude a new diatribe, he said, "Naturally I argued these photos probably resulted from the wiretaps placed on your phone and laptop. Of course, that set me up to explain why that wiretap wasn't reported to the federal prosecutor before Cindy Franklin's death. As for the alleged message exchanges, even the FBI admits those could be fraudulent. They're investigating time stamps currently."

"I'm just screwed, Andy. Dump me before I drag you down."

As he tried to sit next to her on the bed, she pushed him away. "Just leave me alone. I must be a bad seed. Now please, if you have any feelings for me, just leave me alone. Please."

He ambled to the doorway, then turned. "I've arranged for my security team to have someone sit outside your door day and night. I'll also beg Dr. Harrison to overrule those arcane insurance company rules and keep you in the hospital a couple more days. It's safer here. I'll then arrange for you to be brought somewhere safe. Goodbye, Sue, and try to remember I've always loved you."

Chapter 35

When Grace entered his apartment, it was well after his usual nine thirty bedtime. He was awake and sitting in his recliner.

No sooner had she sat down next to him than he said, "Well, did you give them hell?"

"Sure did. We met this time at Annalee Jackson's home, which, by the way, is across the street from Henry Taylor's chateau. He was at our meeting because the board has officially named him executive vice president for health affairs for the entire new comprehensive cancer center. The other folks present were Chairman Cambridge, CEO John Freidman, and their lackey lawyer, Peter Regan."

"OK, so you had a full house. What happened?"

"Well, I sure as hell skipped tea and crumpets and got right to the point. In no uncertain terms, I let them know our demands have doubled—that we demand not only more financial compensation for your injuries but also a larger input on the board, as well as a share of future revenue. Are you aware that their project is expected to cost $1.8 billion? That's *b* for a billon."

Wringing his hands together as if it would force open his densely clawed fingers, Malcolm said, "I had no idea. This is not a hospital addition or even a brand-new building. This is a conglomerate."

"Right on, Malcolm. Turns out they have over three-fourths of the money committed at this point by secret major investors. They expect, as in all new construction projects, the costs will double. But their goals are gargantuan. They want a game changer in cancer care. They plan to build in the Finger Lakes region not only a cancer hospital but also an entire campus and research center devoted to the full spectrum of cancer care. Such care would include nursing homes, family residence facilities, hospice care buildings, full lab support with complete genetic profiling, and a major bioinformatic center to store and share all their latest discoveries. As a compelling top hat to this entire project, they plan to enroll the three central New York universities, each with their own distinguished med schools, as partners. Naturally, this picturesque location in the center of the state would draw patients away from New York City's crime-ridden metro area. It would also attract from Pennsylvania and Canada and would pillage the Buffalo center."

Malcolm said, "So why did they divulge all of this to you tonight? It certainly has been years in planning."

"Indeed, it has been in planning for several years. But they're also privy to some new FBI information that suggests you were the innocent target of a plot by that bitch Whitney, Dreskin, and some unknown pervert."

"So they agreed to your terms?"

"Damn right they did. I made it crystal clear not only that we are prepared to sue for the paltry malpractice dollars but also that we demand restitution for their evil intention to create a false narrative to implicate you and me in a deceitful plan to impede their grand hospital designs. I merely had to play them the recorded conversations with their chairman, vice-chairwoman, and senior board members about how they tried to implicate us in a plot that might have impeded their progress."

Malcolm laughed hard enough to shake his chair. "You smart little lawyer. You mean to say you secretly recorded each of your meetings with them? Which as you know is illegal."

Responding with a howl to match his, she said, "I sure did. Even their lackey lawyer pointed out its illegality. But I countered that in six months, they'll have an official site review from the American Cancer Society. So, I asked, will the Cancer Society reviewers and the *New York Times* chastise me for this secret recording, or will the four cancer centers in New York and Buffalo protest their underhanded conniving ways? Suddenly they saw the wisdom of partnering with us."

"Well done, little sister. All it took was a little bending on everyone's part, and we accomplished our goals: getting revenge on Whitney, solidifying our relationship with Congressman Rye, and assuring our future."

Grace then said, "It's late. I need to get home. Tomorrow I have an early-morning conference call with my LA office."

"But I have an appointment with my plastic surgeon, Dr. Cook, in the morning."

"I know. But I've arranged for your car and a driver to take you to his office, and I'll meet you there." Patting his arm, she said, "You did this before. The nurses will get you to your car. The driver will make the short trip to the office, and Dr. Cook's nurse will escort you into the office through the private entrance. You'll be safe, and I might even get there before you."

Malcolm sighed, then said, "Don't be late."

Chapter 36

After Malcolm arose, he showered and dressed himself. A gratifying aura swept over him for the first time in a long while: he was adapting to his blindness. Perhaps it was the sense of victory that Grace had secured from her meeting with the board of directors. Or perhaps it was the tranquility of knowing that the few missteps he and Grace had made were unnoticed or now forgotten. The knock on his door revealed his caretaker, who delivered his usual breakfast of orange juice, two scrambled eggs, two rye toasts, and blueberry jam. After she spread the jam over his toast, he kindly said, "Thank you. I really appreciate your helping me."

"Mr. Reinhardt, your driver will be here in forty-five minutes. He'll take you to your doctor's appointment. I'll let you know when he arrives, and I'll guide you to the car. Also your sister called to say she's running on time and will meet you at Dr. Cook's office. Is there anything else you will need?"

"No, thanks." Using two hands, he scooped the scrambled eggs onto his toast while looking forward to his morning Starbucks latte with Grace.

Although he was still uncomfortable traveling alone, the knock on his door that signaled it was time to go helped him fortify his courage. As his aide escorted him to the elevator, he concentrated on his breathing. His therapist had taught him that. It was working as it diminished his fear. Exiting by the front door, the fresh morning air and sunshine unclenched the tightness in his chest. Assisting him into the rear seat, his aide secured his seat belt and then smoothly closed the door.

His driver said, "Good morning, Mr. Reinhardt. It's a pleasant day."

"Good morning," Malcolm answered.

As they drove away, Malcolm said, "You're not the same driver I had last time."

"No, sir. That was Peter. He's off today. I'm Larry. Good to meet you, sir."

However, after a few minutes of travel, Malcolm's vague sense that something was different swelled. The typical new car smell wasn't there. But his car was only a couple weeks old and had been driven only once before. Since his blindness, his other senses had become more acute. Then again, so had his sense of paranoia. Sweeping his hand across the upholstery, the vague feeling that it too was different blossomed. The leather was older and worn. After several sharp turns swayed him side to side, he finally said, "Are you taking a different route to Dr. Cook's office?"

"I'm not sure what you mean, sir."

Gruffly he said, "I mean this doesn't seem to be the same way my last driver took."

"I'm not certain which roads he took, but this is the correct route. Perhaps you're noticing a different traffic pattern this morning."

Sternly and more loudly, he said, "Can you please call my sister's cell phone?"

"Sir, I'm driving, and I can't reach over to my phone. Plus it's illegal to use a phone while driving."

"Boy, don't tell me what's legal!" he shrieked. "This car has a built-in phone. Now call her, damn it."

"Sir, I don't have her number."

"The car phone is programmed to connect to her cell."

"But do you have her cell phone on you, sir?"

"Of course not."

"Well, how can I call a number that's on her phone if it's not connected by Bluetooth?"

"Then stop this car and call 911. This isn't my car."

"Sir! Please calm yourself. I was told you're under considerable stress. We're only five minutes away from your appointment. Plus your sister will be waiting for you."

Realizing he wasn't paranoid, he howled, "How did you know my sister would be early? Stop this car now!"

Wildly thrashing his arms, he searched for the door handle. He found it recessed within a small hollow in the door panel, but his clawed fingers couldn't grasp it. At the same time, the car sped up. And the driver's tone went from silky to terrorizing as he said, "Now shut up, you crippled bastard. Sit still, or else I will stop the car and beat the living shit out of you. Which no one will see behind these darkly tinted windows."

Too afraid to speak, too weak to cry out, and too helpless to fight, he folded his arms and only wished he could pray.

After what seemed like an hour, the ride slowed and then stopped. First he heard the front door open, then his. As two hands gruffly hauled him from the car, he stumbled to his knees. It felt like he was on rough tiny stones.

The driver jerked him upright. "Now walk, or I'll drag your ass." After yanking him about two dozen footsteps, the driver said, "Kneel down."

Although his legs felt like clay, Malcolm was too shaken to comply. But a kick behind his left knee buckled him to the ground. Thrashing on the stones, he scraped the heel of his palm. Bringing the wound to his mouth, he licked away a taste of blood. Propped on all fours, he heard the distinct creaking of what sounded like two wooden doors. The driver then hoisted him up like a sack of grain. Pushing, tugging, and booting him, the driver forced him to stumble down what clearly was a ramp. Upon reaching a level area, Malcolm detected an odor that was distinctly musty yet had a tinge of sweetness.

As the driver jerked him forward, he was pushed onto a hard, straight-backed wooden chair.

"Where am I?" he pleaded.

The driver exhaled his foul breath into his face and said, "Where they will never find you."

Moving behind him, the driver jerked Malcolm's arms behind the chair. Then he heard the ratcheting of cold metal cuffs tethering his wrists. This was soon followed by a second set of cuffs that riveted his ankles. As his body thrashed in rebellion, the heavy chair simply wiggled.

As the driver delivered a sharp smack across his scarred face, he said,

"Now if you soil yourself, you'll just sit in it. And by the way, you can scream all you want. No one, and I mean no one, will hear you."

The driver tugged on his wrists and ankles to confirm their security. "I'll be back with more of your friends." With an unpleasant laugh, he said, "It's party time."

As Malcolm sat immobile, he heard bootsteps, then the slamming of those two heavy wooden doors. Although he had been warned, he screeched as loud as he could, "Help, don't leave me!"

Despite the warning, he screamed again and again. Each howl grew louder and louder, but when exhaustion hit him, he was left in darkness, just like in his former hospital bed.

Chapter 37

When Susan Whitney awoke that same morning, she was restless. Yesterday was the last day that Dr. Harrison could cajole her insurance company into extending her in-hospital days. Andy had made arrangements to pick her up and have her stay at his sister's house. This undisclosed location would avoid news reporters and, more importantly, others. Stuffing her few belongings into a clear plastic hospital bag with her unbandaged right hand, she heard raised voices outside her door.

She recognized the deeper male voice as Andy's security person. But she was confused when he lowered his voice and said, "OK, looks valid to me, but I'm still calling her attorney."

The other muffled voice responded, "Suit yourself."

When the door swung open, she matched the voice to Jeffrey Stuhl's face. As he strode toward her with malicious beady eyes and a curled left upper lip, he waved a paper in the air and said, "Susan Whitney, I have a warrant for your arrest." He grasped her shoulders, twirled her around, and commanded, "Put your hands behind your back."

As her anger boiled, she exclaimed, "What the hell do you think you're doing? My lawyer will be here any moment."

As he forcibly bent her forward, she tried to kick him in anatomical parts she assumed were miniscule. This attempt only achieved a burning pain in her surgically wrapped left hand. It also resulted in a knee to her back that flung her prone onto the bed. In seconds, she felt the tight restraint of his handcuffs as he yanked her backward off the bed.

As he babbled words about her civil rights, her rage clotted each word in her ears. While he jerked her toward the elevators, she spotted Andy's security man frantically searching numbers on his cell phone. However, with one last tug and a push, she was inside an empty elevator. Watching the floor numbers click by, she was surprised to see they were headed for the basement. Yanking her out of the elevator, he tugged her toward an open loading ramp. Below the ramp, she spotted two black Crown Victoria cars. The roof of each car was bedecked with a portable dome that flashed a steady red.

As he dragged her down the stairs toward the first car, she howled, "Where the hell are you taking me? And on what charge?"

Opening the rear door, he shoved her inside. As she squirmed to free herself, he swiftly cuffed her ankles. Lying on her back against the rear seat, she scanned the steel grate dividing her from the front. With one last yelp, she said, "Where are you taking me? I want my lawyer now!"

As he turned to leer at her from the front seat, he snarled, "Shut up, bitch. Soon you'll find out where both of you are going."

"What do you mean both of us?"

As his lustful stare scanned her from head to toe, he said with a prurient smile, "Oh, didn't I tell you? Your boyfriend Ray Dreskin is in the car behind us. Soon you'll be together in a very special place."

He laughed as he slammed the gearshift into drive. "Oh, and by the way, I deputized your druggie friend Larry Parnell. He arrested Dreskin." He slammed the accelerator, and she was lurched against the rear cushion as he said, "We've both waited so long to get you alone."

Chapter 38

Andy's anger seethed after his security man reached him. Immediately placing a call to the federal prosecutor, he screeched, "What the hell is going on? You arrested my client before calling me."

"Andy, hold on. Last night we intercepted an email from a Utica, New York, IP address. We tracked it to Larry Parnell. It stated that Parnell and Whitney were planning an escape through Canada. There also was some cryptic info about flying south from Montreal. We were forced to inform the judge, secure the grand jury indictment, and issue an arrest warrant for her, Dreskin, and Parnell. Actually, this entire process was handled by the US Marshals and FBI since Parnell was already on their radar."

"I still should have been called. I should have brought her in. For God's sake, she's still in the hospital. Besides, it wasn't the marshals who made the arrest. My security man said it was your damn Inspector Stuhl."

After a long pause, the prosecutor said, "That's a bit odd. She was scheduled for FBI Agent Monihan."

"So, Louis, again, what the hell is going on?"

Regaining his legal composure, the prosecutor said, "OK, Andy, we know Stuhl is gung ho, but we had to move quickly given the flight risk. Please go to central booking, I'm certain your client is there, and you can help her through the arraignment process."

Canceling yet another appointment, Andy got his car and sped the short distance to police headquarters. Upon arriving there, he had the booking sergeant check the roster. The sergeant stated none of the suspects had yet arrived.

Assuring Andy it could be a traffic delay, he added they would put out a call to the radio cars. Asking Andy to take a seat, he promised to inform him immediately upon her arrival. Plopping onto a hard bench next to a middle-aged couple weeping over their son's accident, Andy had no other choice but to wait.

Grasping at straws, he plucked his cell phone to call Susan's number. Within thirty seconds, the call went to voice mail. In desperation, or perhaps simply to assuage his anxiety, he redialed her number. This time a man answered on the third ring and said, "Hello."

Almost stuttering, Andy said, "My name is Andy Falcone, and I'm trying to reach Dr. Susan Whitney. I'm her lawyer. Is she there?"

In a heavily accented voice, the man said, "I dunno. I'm the hospital cleaning man. I think your lady forget her phone on nightstand. I turn it in to nursing station when done here."

His heart sank as he ended the call. Clearly, she had been pulled away so quickly she'd failed to bring her phone. As a trauma surgeon, she had her cell phone welded to her hip. He even believed it was embedded in her DNA. Something was wrong. He also knew her location was now untraceable. Jumping to his feet, he stepped in front of an elderly woman describing the color of her stolen purse to the desk sergeant.

"Is Dr. Whitney here yet?" he asked briskly. "Please check again."

Excusing himself to the elderly woman, the sergeant frowned and tapped a few keys. He scanned the monitor for several seconds and said, "No, sir. Perhaps she was taken to another precinct. And I really can't check that for you now."

Andy turned and dashed out the front door. He planned to confront the federal prosecutor.

Arriving at the prosecutor's office in record time, he expected to be told to wait. However, when the assistant ushered him directly into the prosecutor's office, Andy expected the worst. Seated at a table next to the desk was Agent Jack Monihan.

"Andy, we have some bad news," the prosecutor said. "I'll have Agent Monihan provide the details."

Monihan folded his hands and frowned. "University police received a radio call over their distress frequency that Inspector Stuhl was overpowered by his two arrest subjects, Whitney and Dreskin. The transmission was somewhat garbled; perhaps he was fighting. But the message suggested a third person was assisting the two suspects. We assume the third person was our fugitive, Larry Parnell."

Andy said, "So what else? Where are they?"

"That we don't know. We located Stuhl's car. It was hit broadside on the driver's side. As I said, both suspects are missing, along with Inspector Stuhl."

"Are there any witnesses to the accident?"

"So far a couple pedestrians saw it and reported that the driver and a handcuffed woman were tossed into the second vehicle, which sped away toward Highway 90, heading east. That's all we have now. Local and state police have a vehicle description and an all-points bulletin. Since Stuhl is armed, we must consider the fugitives as armed and dangerous."

The prosecutor added, "I'm sorry, Andy. You must understand how bad this looks for your client. Assaulting and kidnapping a police officer ups the risk should there be a standoff."

"I tried calling her," Andy said. "Her phone was left at the hospital. She wouldn't have left it if this were a usual arrest. Something is drastically wrong. It doesn't make sense. Sue can be hotheaded, but never this kind of behavior."

Monihan said, "No doubt Stuhl should have let me and the marshals handle this arrest. We probably could have handled the third guy too. Nonetheless, it was a legal arrest warrant, and now your client will be charged with escape, assault, and kidnapping." As an afterthought, he said, "Oh, we tried to track Stuhl's phone, but it was tossed on the road near their accident."

Chapter 39

Following the staged car accident by Stuhl and Parnell, Susan was stuffed into the rear seat of Parnell's vehicle and secured with a seat belt. Gazing over at Ray Dreskin, she recognized a fracture zygoma from the dark blue lump that was expanding laterally to his left eye. With his chin slumped against his chest and blood oozing from his nose, mouth, and ear, she assumed he had sustained a concussion following a struggle.

Glancing at the rearview mirror, she thought the image of Parnell's face resembled that of a crack addict filled with unbridled rage. Too afraid to speak, too afraid to move, she remained frozen and switched her gaze to the back of Stuhl's oily, shoe-black hair.

After driving for what seemed like an hour, they entered a gated community with homes clearly at a price point for America's 1 percent. Pulling up to the coded gate box for entrance to the estates, Parnell turned to Stuhl and said, "Give me the fire-code key."

Stuhl fumbled in his pocket and plucked a key on a ring, which he tossed to Parnell. With a single key turn, the ornate silver double gates drifted open. "Now let's hide this damn car," Parnell said.

Stuhl responded, "Take the driveway for the third house on the left. Follow it to the far end. There're dense woods back there, plus a pond." He chuckled. "So nice of these rich folks to have seven-acre plots of land next to a hundred acres of state-owned green space."

Parnell turned smoothly onto the polished concrete driveway and scowled. "You certain this rich prick ain't home this weekend?"

"I'm pretty sure." Turning to face Whitney, Stuhl said, "Dr. Taylor has a big meeting this weekend. You know, for big-shot executive vice presidents for health affairs. So, Ms. Susan, we should have the entire estate to ourselves to celebrate." He and Parnell snickered. "And why would cops look for us here? We're directly across the way from the vice-chairwoman of your prestigious hospital's board of directors." He paused to give Parnell a high five. "You might even say we're neighbors."

As Parnell weaved farther down the road, which then converted to crushed stone, Susan spotted a clay-pigeon shooting range, complete with spotting towers and clay launchers. In the distance, a faded gray two-story barn resembled one of the typical wine distilleries that dotted many areas in the Finger Lakes. Parnell parked the car beneath a large willow tree whose drooping branches nearly touched the ground, and he killed the motor. Quickly both men flung open the car doors and dragged their prey toward the distillery's sloped wooden doors, which led down a ramp into the basement.

As Stuhl tugged Susan down the ramp, he pulled an overhead chain to a bare hundred-watt bulb, which lit the dank cellar. Susan saw it was filled with assorted furniture and broken wine barrels. As her eyes adapted, she spotted Malcolm Reinhardt secured to a heavy wooden chair. As if Reinhardt could see her, he lifted his head and howled, "Who's there?"

Parnell rambled forward, dragging Dreskin, who barely stumbled. Reaching Reinhardt, he smacked him and said, "Be nice! We brought you friends. Your favorite doctor, Susan Whitney, and your accused plastic surgeon, Dreskin. I bet you wish you could see him again."

As Reinhardt thrashed in his chair and pulled against his cuffs, Susan hollered, "Stop it, Larry. What the hell has happened to you? You're sick and off your treatment meds."

Her plea was rewarded as Parnell dropped Dreskin to the stone floor and strode forward to slap her face. "Listen, bitch, this is no longer your show. From now on, I'll be treating *you*." Pushing her backward onto a stout wooden chair, he secured her handcuffs to the sturdy armrests and her ankle cuffs to the chair's legs.

As Ray Dreskin stumbled trying to stand, both Stuhl and Parnell dragged him onto a third chair and lashed him securely to it.

With the three chairs positioned in a semicircle facing Stuhl, he stood erect and puffed out his chest as if prepared to give a sermon. Then a loud thumping struck the cellar doors. Gazing upward, Stuhl gestured to Parnell and said, "Open the doors. Could be the boss."

Stuhl dropped to one knee and yanked out his service weapon, a Colt .45. He pointed his gun at the doorway as Parnell opened it. A dark figure dressed in a long black leather jacket, matching cowboy hat, and a black hockey face mask descended the ramp.

Sue stared at the figure, who strutted to Stuhl and shook his now unarmed hand with a black leather glove. As they nodded to each other, the figure pointed sequentially to all three prisoners. Stuhl said, "They're all here. Shall we begin the interrogation?"

The figure nodded and pointed to Reinhardt, and Stuhl strode toward him. At the same time, Parnell stood behind Susan and pressed his stubbled face against her swollen cheek. "Soon you'll be next," he said. "And then I'll have you."

Stuhl stood inches in front of Reinhardt, clutched his throat, shook him, and scoffed, "Now listen up, cripple, your boss is here, and it's time to come to the Lord." Stuhl released him. "You were greedy." Spittle flew from his mouth onto Reinhardt's scarred face. "All that money from the hospital for compensation. Who the hell do you think you are?" He jabbed his stubby thumb into Reinhardt's chest. "And being so unreasonable with your good friend Congressman Rye. He made you a kind offer. But no. You wanted more. So now I'm here to reason with you. In front of the boss, of course." He shook Reinhardt's shoulders until the chair almost flipped. "And I brought a little something to jazz you up."

As Stuhl moved away from the chair, Susan watched him attach two jumper cables to a twelve-volt storage battery. Holding a red and a black clamp in each hand, he touched the tips together near Reinhardt's face. The hiss and crackle lit the room almost as bright as the hundred-watt bulb. The sound and perhaps even the heat made Reinhardt scream.

Stuhl then said, "I've learned over the years that prisoners need to feel punishment rather than just imagine it." With that, he planted both electrodes on Reinhardt's chest. He pressed them hard until everyone saw smoke. He snapped them away as Reinhardt's head jerked backward. Stuhl then clutched his victim's hair and shook him awake. "Are we ready to chat now?" he asked calmly.

As if the sight of torture stimulated Parnell, he whispered into Susan's ear, "I hope I won't need to use those on you before you do what I want."

As Stuhl moved away from his victim, he gazed upon his prisoners and said, "Since none of you will ever leave until the boss and I get what we want, I need to give you some facts. The hospital board of directors, Congressman Rye, and many senior business leaders from across the state want to build this profitable cancer center. You assholes, in your own selfish ways, have become impediments to our greater goal. Therefore, you must be dealt with or eliminated. The choice is yours. Reinhardt was offered a sweetheart deal, but alas, he got greedy."

Stuhl began to pace in front of their chairs. "Each of you have been charged with felonies that assure long prison terms. Plus you two assholes assaulted a federal police officer and fled arrest."

As Susan felt her lip beginning to swell, she shrieked, "Let's see if you two perverts can prove that in court. And should you fail, I swear I'll kill both of you."

Parnell raised his fist, but Stuhl waved him off, saying, "Allow me to demonstrate how you will be found guilty in a court of law." He crooked his index finger, summoning Parnell to stand in front of him. Placing both his arms behind his back, Stuhl said, "Larry, as we discussed, punch me in the face two times as hard as you can."

With a snarl and a glare, Parnell punched Stuhl full force on both sides of his face. As expected, Stuhl fell to the ground. He rose, rubbed his jaw, and said, "Well, didn't expect it would be so hard. But I needed it."

Susan glanced at the solitary figure standing stoically still. The hazel eyes staring through the face mask were unflinching.

When Stuhl regained his composure, he extracted a .38-caliber revolver from his waistband. Waving it in front of Susan and Dreskin, he said, "This pistol is unmarked and untraceable. My report will claim this weapon was hidden on Dr. Dreskin when I arrested him. Sadly, I missed it." He smiled. "My bad." He dropped his hand to his side. "But on the way to police booking, Dreskin drew this gun, and with your help, he got me to stop the car and release your cuffs."

"Nice try, mall cop," Susan said, "but how do you explain how your pervert Larry got here? And how he played junior cop to arrest Ray?"

Stuhl lashed back, "Oh, that's easy. As my investigation shows, along with your visit to Cindy Franklin, as well as the emails between you and Larry, you're partners in this crime. But since Larry is a drug addict, a sex pervert, and quite crazy, it's logical that in the midst of our current predicament, the three of you got into a heated argument."

Sue said, "So what the hell does that mean in your illogical brain?"

Stuhl lifted the gun and pointed it at Parnell's head. "Simply this," he said, and pulled the trigger.

The sound shattered the silence of the stone room and echoed off the walls. Reinhardt thrashed wildly as if he were the one who had been shot. Parnell fell backward with a bullet hole though his forehead. He quickly warmed the damp floor with the blood gushing from the exit wound at the back of his head.

"See?" Stuhl said. "Simple. You plotted with a drug addict who was erratic and undependable and became a risk." Seizing Ray's right hand, he wrapped Ray's fingers around the revolver's handle and squeezed to transfer his prints. Next he positioned his own index finger over Ray's, and he fired the weapon into Parnell's body. Then he said, "That evidence should cinch a felony."

Gingerly placing the gun next to Parnell, he turned to Reinhardt and said, "So now, Malcolm, are you ready to confess? You, my crippled friend, are the sole co-owner, along with Congressman Rye, of all the fine property needed to build a critical area within the new cancer center. The congressman demands you sign that property over to him. Is that clear?"

Reinhardt screeched, "Screw you."

Grasping the electrodes once again, Stuhl exploded a cascade of sparks and yelled, "Do we need a little more pain? Perhaps in your private anatomy?" He smacked Reinhardt's face with one electrode. "Or are you ready to sign now? We have all the necessary documents."

Exasperated, Reinhardt capitulated. "All right, no more pain. I'll sign."

As Stuhl jerked a small table in front of Malcolm's chair, the dark figure plucked a document from inside the leather coat. Stuhl placed it on the table, gave Reinhardt a pen, and positioned his hand to sign several pages.

Stuhl then said, "Now that wasn't so hard, was it?"

But to everyone's surprise, Reinhardt howled with laughter as he declared, "The joke's on you, asshole. My signature is meaningless. Directly after my injury, my sister, Grace, got complete power of attorney. Anything I sign must be countersigned by her. So suck it up, buttercup."

With that, the tall dark figure removed the mask and hat and said, "My dear brother, who said I wouldn't sign?"

Chapter 40

Andy Falcone was like a fixture in the federal prosecutor's office. Following the report of Susan's arrest and disappearance, the state police uncovered two witnesses who reported a second black Ford was seen speeding east on Highway 90. Since Larry Parnell had recently rented a run-down apartment in a partially abandoned district in Utica, the marshal service assumed he was there with his captives. However, their subsequent raid revealed nothing other than a collection of pornography, leather straps, and assorted sex toys. They did seize a computer that might uncover clues he believed had been erased on his hard drive.

When Andy pressed for the results of the hard-drive analysis, their response was as expected: it was too early to tell. Parnell's penchant for using the dark web also complicated their efforts to decipher his deleted data.

As Andy brooded in his office, blaming himself for things real and things imagined, his cell phone rang. Caller ID confirmed it was the federal prosecutor.

"Andy, we just received an anonymous tip. The FBI is working on it as we speak. The instructions were to pick up a package at the Monroe Hospital lost and found. The package contained a biohazard disposal bag. Inside were a paper surgical mask and cap and a disposable paper gown. The front of the gown had several bloodstains, and the mask, according to the lab guys, is filled with DNA."

"So how long to analyze it?"

"That's a few days away. But Agent Monihan suspected, from the way the package was left for him, that it came from an employee accustomed to handling infectious material. Long story short, he tracked down a mentally challenged woman who has worked for years in hospital sanitation. She claimed that the mask and gown were worn by Reinhardt's sister the day of Malcolm's attack."

Andy gasped. "Are you kidding me? Why did she hang onto it, and why did she wait so long to turn it in? Is this another wild goose chase?"

"We obviously will check the forensics, but from what the cleaning lady told us, Ms. Reinhardt was extra nasty to her. Supposedly she complained daily how poorly his room was cleaned, and she referred to the lady as 'the retard.'" After a pause, he added, "I guess what goes around comes around.

"Andy, here's something you don't know. And I only divulge this now because we are coming to believe Sue is innocent. We have for some months been running an investigation on various high-profile business investors in western New York. The sting operation is code-named 'Project Good Health.' So far we've discovered significant cash is being funneled through offshore accounts into this new cancer center. We have some concerns about key members of the hospital board of directors, and we found out that Grace Reinhardt and former congressman Rye are having regular meetings with them. As you recall, the congressman has a past conviction for health-care fraud."

"Sure, I know all about Congressman Rye and his quest for a cut-rate national medical lab system. Do we suspect Grace Reinhardt had something to do with Sue's disappearance?"

"Yes, Andy, we do."

"So what's next?"

"We have a full team scanning every contact, and we're trying to locate everyone associated with this project. I'll let you know as soon as we find something."

After an hour had passed, Andy began to pace erratically. He imagined only terrible endings, yet he was powerless to do anything. If he lost Susan, he wasn't certain how he would go on. As his darkness approached a nadir, the ring of his cell phone became an elixir. It was the federal prosecutor.

"Andy, we have something solid. We located Dr. Henry Taylor, who, by the way, is a bit of a wimp. He told us he was scheduled for a conference today, but he wasn't feeling well and stayed home. Earlier today, he thought he heard two gunshots coming from the direction of his shooting range. He didn't report it, because he thought some neighborhood kids had gotten onto the property to potshot the range. The state police air unit flew over his house and spotted with infrared detection a hot car engine hidden near a wine cellar and some woods. The car is a black Ford Crown Victoria."

Before Andy could put together his words, the prosecutor said, "And yes, SWAT units and the entire calvary are racing there now."

Chapter 41

Following Grace Reinhardt's exposure, the entire cellar went silent, except for the dripping of a leaky sump pump in a distant corner.

With an increasing wheeze, Malcolm said, "Why, Grace? Why would you do this to me?"

Inches from his face, she snarled, "Why else, brother? Money! I pleaded with you to join me in LA. Get out of this snow-filled ice bucket. But no. You loved the beauty of the four seasons, spring, the leaves in fall, the lakes. All bullshit to me. With money, you fool, you can buy all this scenic beauty and still live in a vibrant city that doesn't close every good restaurant at ten p.m."

She turned away and prowled around Parnell's twisted body. Pointing at it, she said, "This useless pervert served a purpose." Her voice rose to a howl. "Do you know how long it took to find him, train him, and control him to do our tasks? Everyone is convinced he's the villain. They're searching for him right now, while we are safe here."

Striding back to Malcolm's chair, she screamed, "But you, brother of mine, were no help. No, you were a big shot in a tiny pond. Content with working measly malpractice scams against idiots like that pathetic cosmetic surgeon over there. He's chump change compared to big-ticket malpractice suits in LA." She aimed a finger toward Parnell's body again. "So I needed to link that asshole and his feeble mind to a drug-prone bitch like Cindy Franklin." She leaned into Malcolm's deformed ear. "But you fuckin' blew it. You and Congressman Rye were on the verge of greatness. A national medical laboratory with a potential monopoly on all those medical tests. Tests that are repeated a thousand times a day. Tests that can't be avoided, especially when someone has cancer. Which means money and lots of it, all paid by insurance or someone mortgaging their house." With a snarl, she said, "Who the hell cares? It's money in our pockets. You've got cancer. You're going to die. Let's run another test. If the test is negative or meaningless, it makes no difference. You're a dead man walking. Get another test."

She stood and faced her brother. "You, the great lawyer, lost the congressman's case. And because of it, we all lost money. So I had to dispose of you and speed your wretched wife to her grave. The explosion was intended as a merciful ending. Even Parnell couldn't screw it up. But he did, and you lived."

Pacing away from him, she said in a near whisper, "I did make one mistake. How to end your misery in the hospital? How to get in and out of your room unnoticed? How to be sure the evidence would point to Whitney or that fool plastic surgeon? At first, I planned to inject potassium chloride into your IV. An instant heart stopper. But no, that would set off alarms and flood the room with nurses. It had to be slow, lethal, and, yes, painful, but more importantly, it had to give me time to get out. Since you were hooked to a breathing machine, you couldn't cry out. Plus your thrashing would only trigger alarms that would be interpreted as expected struggles with the respirator. A perfect plan: acid to the eyes. If only I had pointed the needle closer to your nose, the acid would have entered your brain and slowly wiped you out. But alas, the needle pointed toward the ears, and most of the acid flowed down the side of your face."

She halted as if she had had an epiphany. "So what was my only mistake? How to dispose of my cap, mask, and gown. I couldn't walk down the corridor, could I? So I ripped them off and stuffed them into the green trash bin. That would have been OK if that that retard cleaning lady hadn't walked in to clean. She saw me as I walked away. Hopefully that mental defective didn't realize my stuff should have been placed in the red biohazard bin."

Pacing back to Parnell's body, she reached into her black jacket and extracted a set of blue plastic gloves. Tugging them over her hands as if preparing for surgery, she bent down to retrieve the revolver Stuhl had tossed. She snapped around to face Stuhl. "You must understand I can't stake my future on your silence. Although you were promised a vice presidency for hospital security in the new center, you are too vainglorious. Money won't satisfy your need to become a legend."

Instinctively Stuhl swiftly pulled back his jacket to expose his belted weapon. Unfortunately for him, Grace's trigger finger was faster. Again the hollow cellar was filled with echoes as Stuhl clutched his obese gut and fell forward.

Malcolm yelped and said, "Grace, please stop it! Think what you're doing. Your entire house of cards will collapse. Do you think Rye will let you live? He's a beast."

"Oh, come now, Malcolm. Just days ago, you claimed to trust him. But you needn't worry. You won't be around to learn the end."

"Grace, you're my sister," Malcolm pleaded. "Can't you appreciate what I've done for you?"

"My dear brother. Appreciation is an exported commodity. It has no value to those of us seeking profit. Like you did before you became weak. If I allowed you or that idealistic bitch Whitney to live, you'd begin a new phase of your life. A repeated phase within a shit pile on another universe."

Grace strode sharply toward Susan, jabbed the revolver's tip under her chin, and said, "What's the matter, bitch? Have you nothing to say?"

"Yeah, I do. You're a monster that'll burn in hell. Not only are you a killer, but you're a pathetic crook driven to scam sick, dying cancer patients. Don't ever call me a bitch again."

Grace lifted the butt of the revolver to smack Whitney's jaw. It appeared as though, instead of creating a wound, she had turned on the sun. Between each cracked wooden plank forming the overhead doors, light flooded the room. Even the block-glass windows around the cellar became muted spotlights. Next came a piercing explosion, which blew open the doors. In the following second, two flash-bang grenades filled the room with blinding light and ear-bursting sound. Those who had the capacity to see watched six helmeted men aim red laser dots on Grace's forehead. Each dot was a marker for a cascade of hollow-tipped bullets. As one officer knocked Grace to the floor, another disarmed her.

Turning their attention to their traitorous officer, Stuhl, they shouted to paramedics waiting outside. As the medics assessed his wound, each officer was intent on saving his life. For they all knew an eternity in prison for a fallen cop, albeit a fake one, served justice better than death.

Finally, they uncuffed Susan, Dreskin, and Reinhardt. Susan was still shaking, her mind a whirlwind of sound, light, and fear. As they strapped her to a gurney, she slowly felt the cool night air. As her vision returned, she saw flashing lights. And only when she felt the ambulance drive away did she feel safe.

Chapter 42

When Andy entered Susan's hospital room, she was seated upright in bed against two pillows. Other than a couple minor bruises on her cheek, which she may have touched with a dab of makeup, she appeared remarkably relaxed and, to Andy, even beautiful. As Dr. Harrison evaluated her left hand, she spotted Andy and smiled. "Here I am again."

Dr. Harrison, unfazed, continued his examination by palpating and flexing each of her fingers. Then he said, "We can leave the bandages off. You're healing just fine." He turned toward Andy and chided, "I thought I told you to keep her out of trouble."

"Dear doctor, you don't know how much I tried."

Andy moved toward the bed, sat on the edge closest to her, and gently lifted her free left hand. Gazing at Dr. Harrison, he said, "Perhaps this may help."

Turning to Susan, he held out a marquise-cut diamond ring and said, "Sue, many years ago you gave me a ring. Now can I give you this one to marry me?"

She gazed deeply into his eyes, smiled, and said, "Yes."

As he slid the ring onto her finger, she added, "I wasn't picturing myself looking like a mess for this moment. But I've always loved you and will forever." Holding her hand up to admire the ring, she fell forward and embraced him with all her strength. Then she began to cry.

Dr. Harrison, holding back a tear, said, "After all you've been through, *now* you choose to cry?"

As if the bed were a cloud, she rose, clutched his shoulders, and kissed him, and then as quickly buried her head in his shoulder and continued to sob.

Dr. Harrison stood and said, "I've never seen this done in a hospital before, but I'm going to leave and close your door. As chief of surgery, I'll post a sign that says Do Not Disturb.

"And do you know what? From what I just heard from Agent Monihan, CEO Friedman has been arrested along with his golf buddy Henry Taylor. Of course, the worst punishment will befall Grace Reinhardt. Rumor has it the prosecutor wants a death penalty and will accept a life term. Our poor plastic surgeon Dreskin—turns out he was just a pawn greedy for a higher hospital position. And I'm sure you'll be glad to hear Stuhl is upstairs recovering from surgery. He'll live to join Grace with a life term.

"Oh! And by the way, our prestigious board chairman and vice-chairwoman were also arrested this morning. And since they're so eager to sing, it appears there will be a slew of other arrests for greedy investors. So according to hospital bylaws, in such an emergency, I'm totally in charge."

He strutted to the door with pride. Then he turned and said, "I don't think anyone will dare enter this room." Almost as an afterthought, he added, "Do you know how all this trouble began? It's greed. Pure unbridled health-insurance industry greed. Evil arises from people, not companies, which are merely tools. It's individuals who fall from grace simply by bending their professional oath to do no harm."